BEHIND THE BOOKCASE

BEHIND THE BOOKCASE

Mark Steensland

illustrated by Kelly Murphy

Delacorte Press

Text copyright © 2012 by Mark Steensland
Jacket art and interior illustrations copyright © 2012 by Kelly Murphy

All rights reserved. Published in the United States by Delacorte Press, an imprint of Random House Children's Books, a division of Random House, Inc., New York.

Delacorte Press is a registered trademark and the colophon is a trademark of Random House, Inc.

Visit us on the Web! randomhouse.com/kids

Educators and librarians, for a variety of teaching tools, visit us at randomhouse.com/teachers

Library of Congress Cataloging-in-Publication Data
Steensland, Mark.
Behind the bookcase / Mark Steensland. — 1st ed.
    p.   cm.
Summary : Sarah, her brother Billy, and her parents are moving into her deceased grandmother's house for the summer in order to fix it up and sell it, but this is a house of locked rooms and many dark and dangerous secrets.
ISBN 978-0-385-74071-5 (hc) — ISBN 978-0-375-89985-0 (ebook) —
ISBN 978-0-375-98963-6 (glb)
1. Haunted houses—Juvenile fiction. 2. Brothers and sisters—Juvenile fiction.
3. Horror tales. [1. Brothers and sisters—Fiction. 2. Haunted houses—Fiction.
3. Mystery and detective stories. 4. Horror stories.] I. Title.
PZ7.S815313Beh 2012
813.6—dc23
2012010896

The text of this book is set in 14-point Seria.
Book design by Michelle Gengaro-Kokmen

Printed in the United States of America
10 9 8 7 6 5 4 3 2 1
First Edition

For my father

CONTENTS

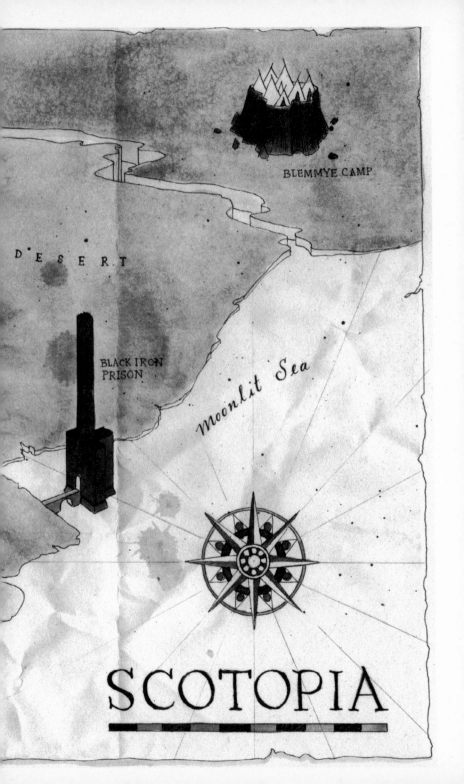

BLEMMYE CAMP

DESERT

Moonlit Sea

BLACK IRON
PRISON

SCOTOPIA

BEHIND
THE
BOOKCASE

CHAPTER 1

Arrival

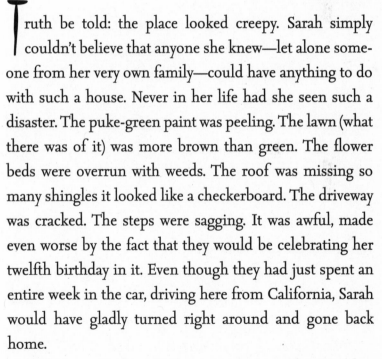

Truth be told: the place looked creepy. Sarah simply couldn't believe that anyone she knew—let alone someone from her very own family—could have anything to do with such a house. Never in her life had she seen such a disaster. The puke-green paint was peeling. The lawn (what there was of it) was more brown than green. The flower beds were overrun with weeds. The roof was missing so many shingles it looked like a checkerboard. The driveway was cracked. The steps were sagging. It was awful, made even worse by the fact that they would be celebrating her twelfth birthday in it. Even though they had just spent an entire week in the car, driving here from California, Sarah would have gladly turned right around and gone back home.

"This is it?" she asked, just to be sure, hoping they had somehow made a mistake, that they had turned onto the wrong street and this wasn't really Grandma Winnie's house at all.

In the front seat, Mom and Dad exchanged a long look and then Dad said grimly, "Afraid so."

Sarah's younger brother, Billy, meanwhile, was wearing a huge smile, which got even bigger when Dad confirmed that this was indeed where they would be spending the summer. "Awesome!" Billy said, with a reverence that thoroughly annoyed his sister.

"What could be awesome about this?"

"Look at it," he said. "It's like a haunted house."

"Billy," Dad said. "Don't say that."

"But it is!" he insisted.

"I'm sure it's just because Grandma wasn't feeling well the last few years. She couldn't keep the house up."

"No, honey," Mom said. "It's always been like this. That's why the bullies called me Creepy Carol in school. Now can you understand why I wanted to leave as soon as I could? And get as far away as possible?"

Dad tried to put his arm around Mom, but she opened the passenger door and got out of the car quickly. Dad gave Billy one last sour look and then got out with her.

"What's wrong with them?" Billy asked.

"This is where Mom grew up," Sarah said. "Her mom

died in there. Do you think she liked hearing you say it looks haunted?"

"Oh," Billy said, his smile suddenly evaporating into a look of timid shame. "I didn't think of that."

"Of course not," Sarah snapped. "You don't think of anyone but yourself."

"That's not true."

"Prove it," Sarah said as she grabbed her backpack and opened her door.

The air outside the car was hot and humid. Where they were from in Southern California, it was hot, but not wet like this. Sarah felt as if her mouth were pressed against a damp towel.

Billy got out of the car behind her and went over to where their parents were standing. "Sorry, Mom," he said. "I didn't mean it the way it came out."

Mom patted Billy on the head. "It's okay," she said with a sniffle. "I understand." She faced the house, shielding her eyes from the sun with one hand. "In a way, I'm glad you like it. At least one of us does."

Mom and Dad turned away and started toward the front door. Billy faced his sister and stuck his tongue out at her. She rolled her eyes and joined their parents on the steps.

Mom fished in her purse until she found a yellow

envelope. After Grandma Winnie had died, Mom had gotten a whole bunch of these yellow envelopes in the mail. When Sarah had asked about them, Mom had explained that they were from lawyers telling her about things she had to do to settle Grandma's affairs. The biggest of all these things was selling the house. That was why they were there. Mom and Dad had decided they would do what they could to fix it up before they sold it. But now that Sarah had actually seen it, she didn't think one summer would be enough time to fix the house. Not unless they rented a bulldozer and just pushed it flat.

Mom opened the envelope and took out a key. While Dad held the squeaking screen door, she put the key in the lock, turned it, and pushed the front door open.

A gust of cool air came out of the darkness beyond and swept over all of them. To Sarah it felt like running through the sheets hanging on the laundry line in their backyard at home. In fact, it felt so much like something—or someone—pushing past her that Sarah gasped a little and stepped back. Was Billy right? Was Grandma's house haunted?

Mom and Dad looked at each other again and Sarah

could tell they had felt it, too. Mom just stood there, as if she were frozen in place.

"Honey?" Dad said. "Are you okay?"

Mom nodded slowly, then turned around. "Sarah?" she said. "You want to go first?"

Sarah shook her head quickly. The cool air wasn't the only thing spooking her. Maybe it was because the June sun was so bright, but the darkness beyond the open front door looked as thick as a pool of swirling oil.

"I will!" Billy shouted, and pushed his way past Sarah and up the steps.

Dad couldn't help but laugh as Billy went in. Sarah didn't think it was funny at all. Instead, she was seized with the desire to grab her brother by the shoulder and pull him back. She was afraid that once he touched the darkness, it would suck him in like a whirlpool. She had to stop him.

But it was too late. He was gone.

A moment later, they heard him inside. "Cool!" he said. Relieved, Sarah pulled her hand back. Mom waited another moment, then stepped over the threshold. Dad faced Sarah. "Come on, sweetie," he said, smiling that big smile of his, the one that always told her everything was going to be okay.

Reassured, she climbed the steps and went inside.

CHAPTER 2

Yellow and Blue

The first thing that hit her was the smell. Sarah had a very strong sense of smell, and right now she wished she didn't. The whole place smelled heavy and thick and dusty, like the old curtains in the school gym. She wanted to say something about it but decided not to. Mom's feelings were already hurt enough by Billy's "haunted house" comment; she certainly didn't need Sarah telling her the place stank, even though it did.

A sudden swishing sound to her right made Sarah think a giant bird was swooping in to attack her. She was so startled that she screamed and threw her hands up to protect herself. Mom broke into a laugh and rushed toward her, hugging her tightly.

"I'm sorry," Mom said, "I didn't mean to scare you. I was just opening the curtains." And now Sarah saw: the curtains in the front windows were made of thick red velvet and hung from heavy brass rings, which sounded like knife blades sliding out of metal sheaths when they slid over the rod.

"Like this," Dad said as he yanked the other curtain open. The swishing sound wasn't nearly so scary now that Sarah knew what it was. She smiled and shrugged.

But then Billy opened his mouth and started singing in a squeaky voice, "Sarah is a scaredy-cat, Sarah is a scaredy-cat." Sarah broke from Mom's hug and lunged at him, but he got behind Dad before she could reach him.

"All right," Dad said. "That's enough of that. Leave each other alone."

Sarah sighed and turned away. With the curtains open, the darkness was half gone and she could finally see the room.

It was huge, but what really grabbed her was that the walls weren't walls at all—they were bookcases. In more than one of her letters, Grandma Winnie had told Sarah about all the books she owned, but Sarah had never imagined that she had been talking about this many. The bookcases reached all the way to the ceiling, and they were stuffed. There wasn't one empty spot. For someone like Sarah, who loved to read, this was heaven.

"Wow," she said quietly.

"Betcha can't say that backward," Dad said. Sarah

grinned and shook her head. He always said that when she said "Wow." And he still thought it was funny every time.

"Are these all yours now?" Sarah asked.

Mom nodded.

"So we can keep them?"

"Of course we can't keep them," Mom said.

"But why not?"

"How would we get them back home?"

"In boxes."

"And where would we put this many books?"

"In my room," Sarah said simply, as if there were no other answer.

"You don't have space for the books you already have," Dad said.

"Then we could build an addition."

"With what money?"

"All the money you're going to make from selling this house."

"That is going to pay for your college. I hope. At least part of it."

"What about my college?" Billy asked.

"Yours, too," Mom said.

"If he lives to see nine," Sarah said under her breath.

Mom raised her eyebrows and Sarah turned away as Dad pulled a book from one of the shelves. A cloud of dust came with it. "Besides," he said, coughing and waving his hand in front of his face, "you don't even know if there's anything here you'd want to read." Then he held the book up into the sunlight and read the title. "Phrenology for Beginners," he said with a laugh.

"What's that?"

"It's the long-forgotten art of telling what kind of person you are by reading the lumps on your head."

"What?" Sarah said.

"You can do that?" Billy asked.

"Of course not," Mom said. "Now let's stop fooling around and get the rest of the curtains and windows open. I think some light and air in here will do a lot of good."

"Agreed," Dad said, and shoved the book back onto the shelf. "You two go upstairs and get everything open. Your mom and I will take care of things down here."

"Deal," Billy said, and started running. Then he stopped short. "Where are the stairs?"

"Over here," Mom called, and Billy started running again.

"Wait for me," Sarah said.

"Why?" Billy asked. "Are you scared the curtains are going to get you again?"

"Billy," Dad said firmly. "Do you need a time-out already?"

"No, sir."

"I didn't think so."

"Come on, Sarah," Billy said, and the two of them dashed to the top of the stairs, then stopped.

The hallway in front of them was shaped like a T, with a closed door at the end of each arm.

"Which way are you going?" Sarah asked.

Billy looked both ways, then pointed to his right. "That way. What about you?"

Sarah swallowed thickly. She knew that it was silly to want to stick with Billy, especially because he was her younger brother. But she had always been . . . cautious. That was the way she preferred to think of herself. She wasn't really a scaredy-cat, was she? Just because she didn't like the dark? Lots of people were afraid of the dark. It was perfectly normal to be afraid of the dark. Billy was the weird one for wanting to rush in everywhere, especially when he didn't know what he might find.

She realized Billy was staring at her, waiting for her answer. She knew that if she went with him, it would just confirm what she was sure he was thinking. So, out of spite more than anything like good sense, she blurted, "I'm going this way," and pointed to the left.

"Really?" Billy said.

Sarah nodded.

"You're not afraid?"

Sarah shook her head.

Billy shrugged. "Okay," he said.

Sarah turned away from him and started toward the door. The light from the window was blocked by the wall, and the door ahead of her was hard to see in the gloom. She squinted, then looked over her shoulder. Billy hadn't moved. He was still standing there, arms crossed, watching her, a smirk on his face.

"What are you waiting for?" she hissed at him.

"What are you waiting for?"

Strangely, her irritation gave her a sudden burst of energy and she spun on her heels, took two steps forward, grabbed the knob, twisted it, and pushed the door open. When she turned around to see what Billy had thought of *that*, she discovered that he was already gone, into the other room. Sarah turned back around and stepped through the open door.

The room was painted bright yellow. The windows above the bed looked down on the neighbor's house to the east, while another window, in a kind of alcove, looked over the backyard. In addition to the closet and a short built-in bookcase, there was a small door in the wall beneath the sloped roof.

Sarah had never seen such a small door before. Curious, she grabbed the knob and pulled. Just inside, she saw a chain attached to a lightbulb. She pulled it to turn the light on, then poked her head through the doorway.

The little room's ceiling slanted down to meet the floor on the far side, about six feet away. She saw boxes full of Christmas decorations at the nearer end, but there was still plenty of room. She hoped her mom and dad would say it was okay to play here, but somehow she was sure they wouldn't.

"Sarah," Billy called. "Come here. Look what I found."

Sarah pulled the chain again, turning off the light, as she stepped out of the room, then closed the door and went down the hallway to the room Billy was in.

Other than being painted blue, it was the mirror image of the yellow room, with the same alcove window, built-in bookcase, and little door. As Sarah had suspected, this was what Billy was yelling about. He stood in front of the short door, holding his hands out like the magician they had seen in Las Vegas on their way here. "Ta-da!" he said when Sarah came in. "I found a secret room."

"I know, Billy," Sarah said, shaking her head. "The other room has one, too. Besides, it's not really a secret, is it? Everyone can see the door." She honestly didn't know how she put up with Billy the way she did. He was so annoying, and not just because he called her a scaredy-cat. He always thought everything was such a big deal. Whenever she said anything about it, her parents told her she had been the same way when she was younger. But she doubted that. There was no way she had ever been so annoying.

She turned to leave just as Dad came in. "Hey," he said. "Look at that, would you? What is that? A secret room?"

Sarah rolled her eyes.

Mom came in behind him. "No," she said. "That's only for storage. Don't play in there."

Dad poked his head through the door and looked around, then pulled it back out. "But why not? It's the perfect size for them."

"Yeah, Mom," Billy said.

"No," Mom said. "I wasn't allowed to when I was a girl." She looked around the room. "I wasn't even allowed in these rooms."

"Why not?"

"I don't know. Your Grandma Winnie seemed afraid of something up here."

"Like what?" Sarah asked, her voice trembling.

"Not anything real," Dad said. "Grandma Winnie was what some people call eccentric."

"That's a masterpiece of understatement," Mom said. "My mother wasn't just eccentric and you know it."

"But what was she afraid of?" Billy asked.

"Nothing," Mom said. "Even if it was something, it doesn't matter now. Let's just get our stuff from the car and have dinner. We have a lot of work ahead of us tomorrow. The sooner we clean this place up, the sooner we can sell it and go back home."

Before anyone could say another word, Mom turned and walked out of the room.

"Is she okay?" Sarah asked.

Dad waited until he heard Mom's footsteps on the stairs and then went down on one knee. "This is hard for your mother in a lot of ways, ones I think maybe even I don't understand. The couple of times I met Grandma Winnie, she seemed perfectly normal. But your mom has told me some pretty weird stories about the things she used to say and do. She didn't want your mom to leave home. She didn't really want us to get married. But after you kids were born, she suddenly got interested in trying to be a family. And I think that upset your mother even more."

"I don't understand," Billy said.

"I do," Sarah said.

Dad nodded to her. "Let's just do what Mom asks and maybe we can get back home sooner than we expect."

Sarah smiled as Dad hugged her and Billy before getting back to his feet and heading downstairs.

The rest of the day went exactly as Mom had said. They unpacked the car, and then, because Grandma's house didn't have anything edible in it, Dad picked up a pizza. By the time they changed the sheets on the beds in the upstairs rooms, Sarah was so tired she almost fell asleep brushing her teeth.

CHAPTER 3

The Unfinished Letter

Breakfast the next morning was a strange affair. Mom seemed in a better mood. But Dad seemed cranky. He kept asking Sarah and Billy if they had heard any noises the night before.

"Like what?" Billy asked.

"Like knocking."

Both Sarah and Billy said they hadn't heard a thing, and Mom finally said, "I keep telling you, it was just the pipes. They used to do it all the time when I was a kid."

"But why aren't they knocking now?"

"I don't know," Mom said. "Can we please just forget about the pipes and talk about my plan for today?"

"It wasn't the pipes," Dad said under his breath.

"Maybe it was Grandma," Billy said.

The room fell silent. Billy looked at Sarah. Sarah looked

at Dad. Dad looked at Mom. Very quietly, Mom said, "It wasn't Grandma."

"Yeah," Dad added quickly, "I'm sure it was just the pipes. Now let's listen to your mom's plan."

Mom took a deep breath, then explained everyone's assignments. First on the list for Sarah and Billy: clean everything out of the upstairs rooms.

"Even the beds?" Billy asked.

"Of course not," Mom answered.

"Not yet, anyway," Dad said, then gave them boxes and tape before sending them upstairs to begin packing. The plan was to have their first garage sale over the weekend, which was only three days away, and for that, they needed to get everything downstairs and sort through it.

Sarah helped Billy tape a couple of boxes together and then left him in the blue room while she went to the yellow room. As she began working, she realized how sad she was that she would never get to see Grandma Winnie again. Grandma had come for a visit after Billy was born, but Sarah had been only three years old, so she couldn't remember anything about it, even with the photos and video her parents had shown her after she asked about it. Grandma had mentioned the visit in a letter to Sarah just over a year before. More letters had followed that first one, and she had often written about how she hoped she could visit again soon or that Sarah would come to her place. Sarah loved getting these weekly letters from Grandma. How sad it was that there would be no more letters; even sadder that Sarah and her family were finally here and Grandma Winnie wasn't. And sadder still was the thought that those letters might have been upsetting to her mother.

Suddenly, Sarah felt a hand run through her hair and she jumped. "Billy!" she shouted, and turned around, expecting to find her brother standing behind her, laughing at his practical joke. But there was no one there. A cold knot of fear formed in her stomach.

"What?" Billy called to her from the other room.

Sarah turned around again, but she really was alone. She stepped to the door and looked across the hall. Billy appeared in the doorway opposite.

"Did you call me?"

"Yeah," Sarah said, not wanting to say anything about being scared. "I was just wondering how it was going over there."

"Good," Billy said.

Sarah gave him a thumbs-up and then went back into the yellow room.

Something was wrong. The chair in front of the strange-looking dresser in the corner had been moved. She was sure that just a minute earlier it had been pushed all the way against the front of the dresser. Now it was at an angle, as if someone had pulled it out for her to sit in. Sarah felt the knot in her stomach tighten. She tried to remind herself what her father had told her about fear. "The only way to overcome something you're scared of," he always said, "is to face it head-on." But this seemed ironic to her now. How could she "face" something that wasn't even there?

"You're being silly," she whispered. "There's no such thing as ghosts." Since she had to clean the dresser out anyway, she moved forward slowly, sat down in the chair, and opened the first drawer.

Expecting clothes, she was surprised to find stacks of paper and boxes of pencils. She opened the next drawer and found boxes of envelopes and stamps. Then she realized that this wasn't a dresser at all; it was a desk. The top part—what she had thought was a drawer without a handle—flipped down to make a writing surface. Behind that, Sarah found even more pencils and pens, along with tiny metal boxes full of rubber bands and paper clips, all squirreled away in cute little cubbyholes. She saw her name on an envelope, and when she pulled it out, a piece of folded paper came with it and floated through the air, moving back and forth as if it were attached to strings and someone was moving it around. After what seemed an impossibly long time, the paper landed on the floor and slid to a stop in front of the short bookcase built into the wall.

Sarah got to her feet, walked over to the paper, bent down, and picked it up. Even before she unfolded it, she could see writing on it.

"My sweet Sarah," the note started out, just like all Grandma's letters did. Sarah scanned the page and then realized the letter was unfinished. The last line on the page stopped in midsentence.

Sarah sat down on the bed to read the letter more carefully. The opening few lines were all the usual inquiries about how school was going and how the rest of the family was. Then the tone shifted. "I'm worried, my dear girl," it said. "Strange things are happening behind the bookcase. I can feel it. And without someone to take over my job watching the doors, I don't know what sort of havoc will come of it. You absolutely must come for a visit as soon as possible. I can't think of anyone else to trust. Never mind what your mother says. You must keep asking until she agrees. I simply don't know how much—"

And that was it.

Sarah frowned. Grandma Winnie had never sounded like this in one of her letters. What "doors" was she talking about? Then she looked at the top of the page and saw that it was dated May 3. That was right around the time Grandma Winnie had died. Was this her last letter? Had she died writing it? Suddenly, Sarah didn't feel so good. She threw the letter back into the desk as if it were on fire, then slammed the top shut.

When she turned around, there was a huge man standing in the doorway. Sarah screamed.

CHAPTER 4

In the Basement

"Whoa!" Dad said. "It's just me."

Sarah caught her breath, relieved that the giant man in the doorway was just her dad. "Don't do that!" she shouted.

"What'd he do?" Billy asked.

"I don't know," Dad said. "And she's not even a teenager."

Sarah rolled her eyes. "Did you want something?" she asked.

Dad nodded. "We've got a load of stuff from the downstairs bedrooms that needs to be moved into the basement."

"Cool," Billy said. "I've been wanting to go down there."

"Me too," Sarah said. Their house in California didn't have a basement, and she was eager to see what one was like.

"Well, good on that," Dad said, and took them downstairs.

He gave each of them a box from the stack outside the master bedroom, then took them through the kitchen and down another set of stairs into the basement.

Sarah was surprised to see that it was already crowded with boxes and furniture.

"Okay, you two," Dad said, "we need to find a place to put these boxes so we can still get through."

"What is all this stuff?" Sarah asked as she moved forward slowly.

"'All this stuff' belonged to your mother's aunt Adeline," Dad said. "Mom says Grandma Winnie inherited it from her after she died and just never did anything with it."

Sarah shook her head and kept walking, Billy close behind her. They wound their way between walls made of furniture and boxes. Past the washer and dryer, they came to a squat black machine with thick pipes shooting out of it in every direction.

"Hey, Dad," Billy said, "what is that thing?"

Dad appeared behind them and squinted at it. "The boiler, I think."

"What does it do?"

"During the winter, hot water from there goes upstairs to those radiators in every room. That's how you keep the house warm."

Sarah continued forward, edging her way around the big black boiler. The space beyond it was dark, and while she hesitated, Billy plunged forward. She thought she could see a door in the far wall and she wondered where it went.

"Hey, Dad," Billy said. "Where does this door go?"

"What door?" Dad asked, pushing his way along the narrow path between the furniture and boxes.

"That one," Sarah said, pointing.

Dad found the chain for the overhead light and pulled it. The bright bulb threw shadows from the boiler across the walls like giant spiders, but they could see the door now. Dad frowned. "Hmmm," he said, "that's weird."

"What is?"

He stared at the ceiling. "That door looks like it's beyond the foundation of the house."

"What does that mean?" Sarah asked.

"Usually basements only go right under a house. Whatever is past that door looks like it goes farther out than it should. And from the looks of that lock, Grandma Winnie didn't want anyone to know what was in there."

Sarah knew what he meant. The lock was so big and old it looked like something from a fairy tale, like the kind of lock an evil queen would keep on her dungeon doors.

"I'll tell you what's behind that door," Mom said, and everyone turned around. She stood at the bottom of the stairs, a box in her hand. She set the box down and walked toward them slowly. "It's a place called Penumbra."

Dad laughed. "Penum-who?" he said. Billy thought this was very funny and he laughed extra hard.

"Don't laugh," Mom said. "Penumbra is where the souls of the dead go to sleep."

Billy stopped laughing abruptly, as if someone had hit his Off switch. "You're kidding, right?"

"Of course she's kidding," Dad said. "But I don't think it's very funny."

"I don't, either," Mom said. "But that's what Grandma Winnie used to tell me."

"Really?"

Mom nodded. "I had forgotten about it," she said. "She used to tell me all kinds of stories. Stuff she read in those books upstairs, I'm sure. Like how this house was full of secrets and doors to places with names I can't even remember now. Things she said that I couldn't understand then, but that I would someday."

"Things behind the bookcases, too?" Sarah asked.

"Yes," Mom said. "How did you know that?"

"One of her letters."

"I don't remember that."

Sarah shook her head. "One she didn't send."

"You're not making any sense."

"I think that runs in the family," Dad said, and Mom raised her eyebrows at him.

Sarah explained about finding the unfinished letter upstairs, and both Mom and Dad shook their heads.

"Now, that sounds like something more than just eccentric," Dad said.

"What do you mean?" Sarah asked. "Like Grandma was crazy or something?"

"Maybe," Mom said. "The stories she used to tell certainly were. And sometimes I think she believed them a bit too much."

"So that's not really Carumba back there?" Billy asked.

Mom laughed. "Penumbra," she said.

"And no," Dad put in quickly, "there aren't any sleeping dead souls back there."

"Oh," Billy said with great disappointment.

Sarah rolled her eyes. "So what is back there?"

Mom shrugged.

"We'll find out soon enough," Dad said.

"What do you mean?"

"It means that if we can't find the key to that lock, I'll have to go to the hardware store and get some bolt cutters."

"What are those?" Sarah asked.

"Like big scissors. Only for locks."

"Why would we need those?" Mom asked.

"We can't sell a house with a locked door in it," Dad said. "Any realtor is going to ask that it be opened anyway, so let's get it over with. What are you worried about?"

Mom sucked in a deep breath. "I don't know. I guess it's just my childhood coming back up on me. My mother really used to scare me with all those stories."

"That explains a lot," Dad said, then playfully nudged Mom in the side and pulled her toward the stairs. "All right," he said, "let's have some lunch. I'm starved!"

CHAPTER 5

The Bookcase Moves

All during lunch, Sarah couldn't stop thinking about what Mom had said about that door in the basement. About how Grandma had told her this house was full of secrets. She knew that it was silly. They had to be stories. But if they were just stories, why had that unfinished letter sounded so serious?

Standing now in the doorway of the yellow room, Sarah knew there was only one way to find out. Afraid that the rest of her family might think she was losing her grip on reality the way they thought Grandma Winnie had, she closed the door and then walked to the bookcase.

It was small, maybe four feet high by two or three feet wide, about the same size as the little door to the storage area. Quickly, she took the books off the shelves and put them into empty boxes.

"This is silly," she whispered. But she couldn't help

herself. She had to know. She took a deep breath and then, carefully, she put one hand on the middle shelf and pulled.

Nothing happened.

She examined the edges of the bookcase, where the molding met the wall, but it seemed as solid as could be. She knelt down and felt along the bottom edge. Nothing. With her hand still on the middle shelf, she pushed herself to her feet. As she did, she heard something snap. She pulled her hand away fast, worried that she had broken the shelf. She knelt again and looked but couldn't see any place where it was broken. She got to her feet and pushed, more gently this time. She heard the snap again and now saw that the top edge of the bookcase was coming away from the wall. She put her hand above the space and felt cool air rushing out. Slipping her fingers into the crack, she pulled a little bit, and to her surprise, the whole bookcase started to slide out of the wall.

"No way," Sarah whispered, suddenly overcome with excitement. She almost called Mom to come quickly and see that Grandma had been telling the truth, but she stopped herself. Not yet, she thought. Not until I get a chance to see what this is all about.

Sarah grabbed the middle shelf like a handle and pulled straight out. The bookcase came out of the wall, scraping over the floor, and Sarah sat down with a loud thump.

"What's going on up there?" Mom yelled from downstairs. "Are you okay?"

"Yes," Sarah yelled back. "I just dropped a box."

Sarah stood quickly and listened to make sure Mom wasn't coming upstairs. Then she pulled the bookcase out just a bit more. The space behind it was completely dark, and the cool air that rushed out over her face felt good in the summer heat.

Sarah still couldn't believe it. This was like something from one of the mysteries she liked to read so much. She had her dad to thank for that—he also liked to read mysteries. He'd started when he was a kid, with books about the Hardy Boys and the Three Investigators. When Sarah had been Billy's age, her dad had read those same books to her. She had become so obsessed with being a detective that her parents had given her a whole collection of investigation gear on her last birthday.

Quickly, she went to her backpack and dug around inside until she found the detective stuff: walkie-talkies, a magnifying glass, an invisible-ink pen, and a flashlight. When she found the flashlight, she turned it on and went back to the bookcase.

She shined the light into the dark space and saw wooden walls that looked very much like those in the storage room behind the short door. But this room was a *real* secret room.

She was sure even her mom didn't know about it. If she had, she would have told Sarah and Billy about it just to tell them to stay out. Maybe that was why Grandma Winnie hadn't let Mom in these rooms when she was a kid. Sarah decided she would explore this secret room later, and then maybe, just maybe, she would tell her mom and dad about it, depending on what she found.

She switched off the flashlight and set it on the floor. Then she lined up the bookcase and used her feet to push it back into the wall. When it was all the way in, she stood up and ran her fingers around the edges. It was just like before. No one would be able to tell it had ever been out of the wall.

CHAPTER 6

Behind the Bookcase

After dinner, Sarah took a shower and dressed in her pajamas. She brushed her teeth, then went into the yellow room. She saw that her bedtime was still half an hour away, but she went ahead and got into bed. This proved to be a mistake. When Mom came in to check on her, she frowned.

"You're not going to bed already, are you?" she asked.

"I'm tired," Sarah said.

"Okay," Mom said. "But you sure don't seem tired. Tell you the truth, you seem just as energetic as you are on Christmas morning."

"I'm just so excited about this place."

"Since when?"

"I don't know. Since now. I'm actually having a lot of fun."

"You're having fun cleaning?" Mom's frown deepened

as she felt Sarah's forehead. "Are you sure you aren't sick?"

Sarah laughed. "Yes, I'm sure."

"Okay," Mom said, and kissed her. "Good night, then."

"Good night."

Mom switched on the night-light, switched off the lamp, and then went out the door. As she was pulling it shut, she said, "Tell me when to stop."

"You can close it all the way," Sarah said.

Mom poked her head back inside. "Are you sure?"

Sarah usually liked to have the door open a little bit. Tonight, however, she needed it closed if she was going to explore the secret room and not get caught. She nodded. "I'm sure."

"Okay," Mom said, and closed the door all the way.

Sarah waited, listening. A few minutes later, she heard Dad put Billy in bed and say good night to him. Then she heard her parents switch off the light in the hallway and go downstairs. She waited for what seemed like an hour, then carefully pushed the covers back and got out of bed.

When her feet touched the floor, it creaked and she froze. She was sure that if Mom and Dad heard her creaking around in her room, they would come up to check on her. She knew it would be best if she waited until the middle of the night when everyone was actually asleep, but she couldn't—she was simply too excited.

She thought she could hear them talking, but then she heard singing and she realized they were watching TV. Sarah smiled. With the TV on, they wouldn't be able to hear her if she was careful and didn't creak too much.

She put on her slippers, then got down on her knees and lifted the bed skirt. She had put her detective stuff in a box under the bed that afternoon in preparation for this moment. Now she pulled the gear out and took it with her to the bookcase.

Even more carefully than she had earlier, she grabbed the middle shelf and slid the bookcase out of the wall. This time, she kept pulling until there was enough space for her to fit behind it. She picked up the flashlight, turned it on, and shined it into the darkness.

As she crouched in the entrance, fear suddenly fluttered through her stomach and her mouth went dry. The cool air that had felt so good on her face earlier chilled her now, and she shivered. She was beginning to think this wasn't such a good idea. What if there were spiders? Worse, what if there were rats? Sarah leaned back. Maybe she should just wait until tomorrow morning.

"No," she whispered. She knew she would never be able to wait. If she didn't go in now, she wouldn't be able to sleep.

She shined the flashlight across the walls again. She saw clusters of spiderwebs, but no spiders. When she shined the flashlight straight ahead, she couldn't see a wall on the far side. She would have to go in if she wanted to find out how big the room was.

She inched forward and pointed the flashlight straight up. The ceiling was far away, much farther than in the storage closet. She could actually stand up in this room. She took a deep breath, went all the way through the entrance, and stood up. She rubbed her shoulders, trying to warm up. She thought about going back for a sweater, but then decided to explore a little bit more first.

She shined the flashlight across the floor and saw that it was unfinished. Splinters stuck up in a few places, so she was glad she was wearing her slippers.

She took another few steps, using the flashlight to check the ceiling and walls for spiders or webs. With her head tilted back, she didn't see the hole in the floor.

Her foot landed on nothing but air and she fell forward with a yelp, tumbling through the darkness.

CHAPTER 7

In the Forest of Shadows

Sarah was asleep and didn't want to wake up, but someone kept tapping her on the shoulder. And they weren't being very nice about it, either. In fact, it felt like they were hitting her with their fist. "All right, all right," she said as she opened her eyes and rolled over. Her head hurt and when she sat up, she felt dizzy. For a moment, she thought she saw a giant hand standing in front of her. She bowed her head, rubbing her eyes. She thought that when she opened them again she would see her mother instead of the giant hand, but the hand was still there.

Sarah gulped. It was the biggest hand she'd ever seen, at least as tall as her dad. Instead of an arm below the wrist, however, this hand had a pair of normal-sized legs with normal-sized feet. An eye as big as a dinner plate blinked at her from the center of the palm. She suddenly realized that if the hand wanted to, it could make a fist and squash her

like a bug. She backed up quickly, her fingers digging into the ground beneath her as she tried to get away. But when the hand just stood there, she stopped, feeling somewhat relieved.

She sat still for a long moment, waiting for the hand to say something to her. But it didn't.

"Who . . . or what . . . are you?" she asked.

The eye blinked once, slowly, but the hand did not answer. And then, all at once, she realized the problem and nearly laughed out loud. "Oh, I'm sorry," she said, covering her mouth with her hand, trying to hide her laugh. "I didn't notice you don't have a mouth." The hand didn't have a nose or arms, either, for that matter. The eye blinked at her again. Then the hand turned around slowly and the fingers closed on the palm three times fast. Now it was Sarah's turn to blink. She scratched her head. "You want me to follow you?" she asked. But the hand just walked away, down a narrow path of black sand between dark trees.

As she got to her feet, Sarah rubbed her head. She had been so scared by the hand and then so relieved it hadn't crushed her that she hadn't had time to really think about what was going on. She looked around and saw that she was surrounded by black trees and black sand. Her first thought was that this must be Penumbra, but she didn't see any sleeping people—alive or dead—so maybe it wasn't. Mom had said there were other places, too, hidden in the house, places with names she couldn't remember. Maybe this was one of those places. Sarah certainly hoped so.

She reached out to touch one of the trees, but her hand

went through the trunk, as if it was the shadow of a tree instead of a tree. Behind her, she heard a rustling, like a silk dress rubbing against itself, and when she looked over her shoulder, she saw a stream of silver water flowing between the trees.

Mesmerized by the bright water, she stepped toward the stream, her eyes tracing its path to where it spilled down the face of a black mountain rising behind the forest. Just above the treetops, she saw a hole in the side of the mountain and suddenly remembered tumbling through the darkness from the secret room behind her bookcase.

She stopped for a moment, thinking this must be a dream. She closed her eyes and rubbed them open, but everything was the same.

She peered up at the hole in the side of the mountain. She could barely see it now. It looked more like a shadow than anything else.

She heard a loud noise behind her, and when she turned, she saw the hand snapping its fingers and motioning for her to follow it.

"I'm coming," she said. "It's just that I've never seen

anyplace like this before." Sarah caught up with the hand, then looked over her shoulder. "I didn't even know a place like this existed. Or that there were . . . things like you." The hand looked at her and the eye blinked. "I wish you could tell me where I am." But the hand kept walking.

Farther along, the stream flowed close to the path and Sarah stopped. She had never seen water so bright, and she bent down to scoop up a handful. She giggled. It was the lightest stuff she'd ever felt—like cotton candy made of ice water—but it wasn't wet at all. It ran through her fingers quickly, except for a single drop that remained in the middle of her palm. She lifted her hand to her nose and sniffed. The drop of whatever it was smelled like nothing. Without thinking, she dipped her tongue in it and winced. It was sharp and cold, like licking a knife, and she shivered as she got back to her feet and ran to catch up with the hand.

As they continued along the path, she looked at the sky, but there were no stars. It seemed close, too, like a dark blue blanket pulled over the top of a box. "Are we underground?" she asked the hand, then shook her head and added quickly, "I'm sorry, I keep forgetting you can't tell me anything. You can't even tell me where we're going. I hope you're taking me to someone who can. You're a nice hand, aren't you? I sure hope you are."

She squinted at the landscape around her, hoping for the sight of something other than black sand and trees. At last the path reached a clearing, in the middle of which stood a long cabin, its windows glowing with orange firelight and a thin trail of smoke rising from its crooked chimney. The whole cabin looked like it was made of rock from the black mountain behind the forest. In spite of that, the orange light and sweet-smelling smoke made Sarah think it must be cozy and warm inside.

The hand crossed the clearing and stopped outside the cabin, where it knocked on the door with its index finger, then stepped back, using its thumb to push Sarah onto the porch.

"Hey," she said. "Didn't anyone tell you it's not polite to push?" But the hand just blinked at her. She straightened her pajama top and faced the cabin door, which was open now. But no one was there.

"Down here," a tiny voice said, and Sarah looked toward the floor, where she met the gaze of a fat black cat.

"Did you say that?" she said.

"You see anyone else?" the cat asked.

Sarah giggled. She couldn't think of anything else to do. And then she realized she wasn't scared at all anymore. How could she be? This was the most amazing thing that had ever happened to her. "I hope you can tell me where I am," she said.

The cat looked at the hand, then back at Sarah. He stepped toward her, sticking his nose in the air and sniffing. "You mean to tell me that you really don't know?" he asked.

Sarah shook her head. "I just hope it's not Penumbra."

"What do you know about Penumbra?"

"It's the place where all the souls of the dead go to sleep," Sarah said.

The cat laughed, a strange laugh, deep and rich. It seemed too big to be coming from a cat, even if he was sort of fat. "No, no, no," the cat said. "Who told you that?"

"My mother," Sarah said sheepishly.

"Well, your mother doesn't know what she's talking about."

"So Penumbra isn't where the dead go to sleep?"

"No."

"Is this Penumbra?"

"Wrong again."

"Then where am I? What is this place?"

"Why," the cat purred, "this is where shadows come from."

"I didn't know shadows *came* from anywhere."

"Oh, but they do," the cat said. "Right here. Actually, from over there." He lifted a paw and pointed. "That's where we grow them. It's called the Forest of Shadows."

Sarah looked at the trees behind her, then faced the cat again. "So that's what this place is called? The Forest of Shadows?"

The cat shook his head. "Just over there. Everything together is called Scotopia."

"Oh," Sarah said. "And who are you?"

"My name is Balthazat, and I am the King of the Cats."

"The King of the Cats?" Sarah said. "I didn't know cats had a king."

"Then you're learning quite a lot tonight, aren't you? Why don't you come in and have some hot chocolate. You do like hot chocolate, don't you?"

"I do," Sarah said.

"Good work, Lefty," Balthazat said to the hand. "Now go make sure none of the sentinels followed you."

The hand blinked.

"Thank you, Lefty," Sarah said, glad to know the hand had a name. "Goodbye." She waved at the hand and it waved back, after which Sarah turned on her heels and went through the door into Balthazat's cabin.

CHAPTER 8

The King of the Cats

The inside of Balthazat's cabin was just as cozy as she had hoped it would be. The light felt even warmer and the smoke smelled even sweeter, like maple syrup. The place was filled with overstuffed furniture, the arms and cushions of which had been used for scratching so many times the stuffing poked through. A big bearskin rug lay on the dark wood floor in front of the fireplace. The dining table was set for four, but there was a different dish at each place. At one was a plate of chicken; at another, salmon; at the third, milk; and at the fourth, a turkey leg. Sarah smiled as she took it in. "Is this all for you?"

"Of course," Balthazat said.

"You really are the King of the Cats, aren't you?"

"Would I make up something like that? Now sit down so we can talk."

Sarah sat in a rocking chair by the fireplace, pulling

herself toward the fire so she could warm up. "But who does all this for you?"

"His name is Jeb."

Sarah nodded. "Is he here now?"

Balthazat nodded, then jumped onto the hearth and came closer to Sarah, lowering his already tiny voice to a whisper. "When he comes in, don't be afraid. He's not the nicest-looking boy, but he's perfectly harmless."

Sarah frowned. "What do you mean by that?"

"You'll see," Balthazat purred, then turned, snapping his tail. "Jeb," he called out.

A moment later, a door at the back of the cabin opened and a boy of about thirteen stepped through quietly. At first Sarah thought half his face was in shadow, but then she realized that it wasn't just in shadow, it *wasn't there*: half of his face was gone. Sarah turned away, feeling as if she had seen something she shouldn't have.

She felt Balthazat staring at her. "Two hot chocolates, Jeb," he said. "I'd like marshmallows and whipped cream." He put a paw on Sarah's knee. "How about you?"

Sarah looked at him. "Oh," she said, "yes, please. The same."

Jeb nodded and disappeared back the way he had come.

"So was I right?" Balthazat asked. "Or was I right?"

"Even so," Sarah said. "It's not his fault he's like that."

"Isn't it?"

"What's that supposed to mean?"

"Just that it is his fault he looks like that. He lost half of his face in a bet."

Sarah felt very confused. "How can you bet your face?" she asked.

"You can bet anything when you play with the blemmyes."

"What's a blemmye?" Sarah asked.

"Strange creatures," Balthazat said, "with heads below their shoulders, in the middle of their chests. Terrible cheaters, too. I tried to tell Jeb that, but he wouldn't listen. Good thing he didn't play double or nothing, eh?" he said, and laughed.

Sarah suddenly felt very uncomfortable. There was something about Balthazat's attitude that bothered her. It was as if he thought he was better than everyone else and he didn't try to hide it. Maybe that's the way it is when you're king, she thought, but I don't like it. "That's not very nice of you," she said.

"Oh, you're right, of course," Balthazat said. "I'm sorry. Do you forgive me?"

"I suppose," Sarah said. She felt confused again. Now he seemed truly sorry.

"Good," Balthazat said. "Because I want us to be friends."

"Friends?" Sarah said, surprised. "How can we be friends? You haven't even asked me my name yet."

"Oh, dear," Balthazat said. "You're right again. I don't know what's wrong with me tonight. I guess I'm just so excited to have a special visitor like you. One who's never been here before, I mean. Well? What's your name?"

"Sarah."

"Sarah what?"

"Sarah Marie Steiner."

"Very nice to meet you, Sarah."

"Nice to meet you, too," she said.

The door at the back of the cabin opened again and Jeb came through with a tray that held two white ceramic bowls filled with so much whipped cream and so many marshmallows, Sarah couldn't even see the hot chocolate. Sarah watched Jeb set one bowl on the hearth; the second he put on a low table next to the rocking chair. "Thank you," she said. Jeb nodded, then turned to Balthazat. With this closer view, Sarah saw that the top of Jeb's head was normal, but the left side of his face was missing, just below his eyebrow all the way down to his chin. It occurred to her that what he looked like more than anything else was a jigsaw puzzle with a piece missing. She wondered if he could talk, with only half a mouth.

"That will be all for the moment, Jeb," Balthazat said.

Sarah watched as Jeb went silently through the door again. When she turned back to Balthazat, he had buried his whole face in the whipped cream and was licking it up as fast as his pink tongue could go. "Delicious," he said.

Sarah gasped. What was she thinking? This had to be a dream. Giant hands and talking cats? A boy with only half a face? It was all simply too unreal. And as much as she wished it wasn't a dream, she was suddenly sure that at any moment, she would find herself back in her bed with the bookcase in the wall and her mom standing over her telling her to wake up.

Balthazat stopped eating his whipped cream and raised his head. For the first time, Sarah noticed that his eyes weren't like a normal cat's eyes. The pupils were round, like a human's. "What's wrong?" he asked.

"I was just thinking that maybe this is all a dream. I really hope it isn't."

"Oh, it's not," Balthazat said. "Would you like me to prove it to you?"

Sarah nodded and Balthazat suddenly shot one paw out and scratched her arm. "Ow," Sarah said, pulling her arm away and rubbing it. "What'd you do that for?"

"You wanted me to. To prove you're not dreaming. Now drink your hot chocolate and tell me where you came from and how you got here."

CHAPTER 9

Quite a Story

In between sips of what proved to be the best hot chocolate she had ever tasted, Sarah told Balthazat she was from California but that her family had come to Pennsylvania because her grandma had died and they were fixing up her house to sell it. She told him how she had discovered the secret room. Balthazat seemed especially interested when she told him about the basement and the big door she had seen behind the boiler, the one her mother had said went to Penumbra. Then he finished his hot chocolate and sat on the hearth, licking one paw and dragging it over his head and ears and mouth, purring the whole time. When Sarah finished, he stopped licking and looked at her.

"Quite a story," he said. "You say your grandma used to live in the house?"

"That's right."

"I see," Balthazat said. "Well, it sure sounds like a nice place."

"It is." She drank the last of her hot chocolate and smiled slowly as she wiped her mouth with her sleeve. "You should see it," she said dreamily.

"I would very much like to," Balthazat said. "In fact, I was thinking that maybe you could take me home with you."

Sarah's eyes widened. "Really? For real?"

Balthazat nodded. "But what will you tell them?"

"Who?" Sarah asked.

"Your mother and father. What will you tell them about where I came from?"

"I'll tell them you came from here, of course." In fact, she couldn't wait to tell them. She was sure that Mom would be relieved to discover that Grandma Winnie hadn't been making things up after all, and certainly was not crazy. This would prove it. Sarah was so excited that she decided she would even tell Billy about this place.

"No, no, no," Balthazat said, and laughed. "You can't tell them that."

Sarah shook her head. "Why not?"

"Because this is our secret." Balthazat jumped into her lap and then crawled onto her shoulders. He rubbed his body against her neck and lowered his voice to a whisper.

"Imagine if you told your mom and dad about this place. First of all, they wouldn't believe you. You know how grown-ups are, don't you?"

"What do you mean?" Sarah asked.

"They never believe anything kids say."

"I guess so."

"Furthermore," Balthazat said, purring again, "even if you proved Scotopia was real by bringing them here, what do you think they would want to do?"

"Show it to all their friends?" Sarah said.

Balthazat nodded. "And then what would happen?" He rubbed his black nose against her cheek. "Those friends would show their friends, and then it wouldn't be a secret anymore. They would form some kind of tourist company to bring even more grown-ups here on trips, and they would trample the forest and throw their trash in the stream and it would be ruined."

Sarah felt herself sagging. "I suppose you're right."

Balthazat jumped to the floor and turned around,

flicking his tail in a series of short jerks. "Of course I'm right. The king is always right. Don't you know that?"

Sarah shrugged.

"So the only way we can prevent such a catastrophe from happening is to keep this place a secret. To do that, you must tell your mother and father that you found me outside, hiding in the bushes, in spite of how undignified that will be for me, the King of the Cats."

Sarah sighed. "I can't tell *anybody* the truth, can I?"

Balthazat shook his head. "That's what a secret is."

"But you're a talking cat."

"Not when anyone else is around I won't be."

"Aww," Sarah said, very disappointed.

"Come now, you and I will still be able to talk. As long as we're alone."

Sarah nodded. "Okay. But what about all this?" She waved her arm at the furniture and plates of food. "I won't be able to give you all of this."

"Oh, I know that," Balthazat said. "This will still be here waiting for me when I come back. Jeb will take care of it."

"You mean you're not going to stay with me?"

"No, no, no. I didn't mean that at all. I meant that Jeb will take care of the cabin until we come back to visit. Won't that be fun?"

Sarah nodded excitedly. The thought of having a place

like Scotopia to visit anytime she wanted—especially with her very own talking cat—was just too much. "So when do you want to go?"

"We have to wait until Lefty comes back," Balthazat said. "Until then, would you please scratch my head?"

Sarah nodded, and as she rubbed her fingers through Balthazat's thick black fur, he purred with delight.

After a few minutes, the door at the rear of the cabin opened and Jeb came in again. Balthazat twisted out from under Sarah's hand. "Thank you, dear," he purred at her.

As Jeb collected their empty hot-chocolate bowls, Sarah caught his eye and their gazes locked for a long moment. His eye was as dry and dark as an empty birdbath, and as sad. Sarah's excitement was suddenly gone. She felt very bad for Jeb. It was the same feeling she got when she saw people who lived on the streets. She wanted to help him in some way, but she had no idea how.

Before she had a chance to say thank you, he turned away quickly. As he rushed back to the door, Balthazat hopped down and followed him.

"Where are you going?" Sarah asked, and stood up.

"I'll be right back," Balthazat said. "You wait there."

Sarah sat down again. Balthazat jumped onto a long table near the door and said something she couldn't hear. Jeb stopped next to him. His shoulders sagged and he faced

Balthazat. The cat looked at Sarah, then said something to Jeb in a hissing whisper. Jeb seemed upset by whatever Balthazat was telling him. All at once, Balthazat swatted Jeb's ear and hissed again. Sarah didn't know what was going on, but it didn't seem right for Balthazat to treat Jeb like that, even if the boy was his servant. She stood up, but before she could cross the room, there was a loud tapping at the door and Balthazat looked at her. "Would you mind getting that for us, dear?" he said.

Sarah opened the door and saw Lefty standing on the porch. "Oh, hi, Lefty," she said, and waved. The hand waved back and blinked at her. "Do you want to come in?"

"No, no, no," Balthazat said. "I'm afraid he's not allowed inside." Sarah looked over and saw the cat running toward her. Behind him, Jeb stood with the tray in his hand, staring at her as if he desperately wanted to say something. But then he turned away and went through the door.

"You certainly have a lot of rules," Sarah said.

"That's part of what a king does."

"What were you saying to Jeb just now?" she asked.

"I told him that I was going away and that he would have to take care of the cabin while I was gone."

"What did you swat him for?"

"It's really none of your business. But since I want us to be friends, I'll tell you. I told him I was leaving and he said I couldn't. I simply had to remind him who makes the rules around here. Don't your mother and father spank you when you break their rules?"

"No," Sarah said.

"No?"

"They give us time-outs."

"Us?"

"Me and my brother, Billy."

"Ah. Well, at least they have some sort of discipline." Balthazat faced Lefty. "Well? Is the coast clear? No sentinels?" Lefty turned around and stepped down from the porch. "Excellent," Balthazat said. He looked at Sarah.

"Are you ready to go? Shall we have Lefty take us back to where he found you?"

Sarah nodded and closed the door after Balthazat trotted past her. Together, the three of them stepped into the clearing and headed toward the forest.

CHAPTER 10

Second Thoughts

"So what's a sentinel?" Sarah asked.

"They're like guards," Balthazat said. "They patrol the forest and make sure that no one like you gets in. You're lucky Lefty found you before one of them did."

"You mean I'm not supposed to be here?"

"That's right."

"Why not?"

"For the same reason you can't tell your parents about this place. Because then it wouldn't be a secret anymore."

"What would they do if they caught me?"

"Take you to the king, I suppose."

"Isn't that you?"

"No, no, no," Balthazat said. "I'm just the King of the Cats. Even I have a king. The one who rules all of Scotopia. And that is who the sentinels would take you to."

"What's his name?"

"Nobody knows."

"Where does he live?"

"Nobody knows that, either. Except the sentinels, I suppose. For everyone else, visiting the King of Scotopia is a one-way trip."

Sarah felt a sudden tug of fear. "Is that why you're scared of the sentinels?"

"I'm not scared of the sentinels," Balthazat said, practically spitting the words. "I just don't want our fun to be spoiled, that's all. If they caught me with you, we'd have double trouble."

"What do you mean?"

"The breach is not to be crossed in either direction."

"I don't understand."

Balthazat sighed. "You aren't supposed to be here and I am not supposed to go where you came from. But I won't let that stop me."

"Oh," Sarah said, and looked away from Balthazat, into the shadow trees. She began to feel guilty and wondered if she should still let him come with her now that she knew it was against the rules. Trouble could mean punishment. She didn't like it when her parents punished her. And she certainly didn't like the sound of being punished by the King of Scotopia.

Balthazat stopped and put his front paws on her

knees. "Don't tell me you're having second thoughts," he said.

"Well . . . ," Sarah said, looking down at him and twisting her hair the way she always did when she had a difficult decision to make.

Balthazat dropped to all fours again. "Aren't you the high and mighty one," he said, pacing back and forth in front of her, his tail flicking angrily. "Didn't you tell me you weren't supposed to play in that secret room? And you did anyway, didn't you? Now that you've had your fun breaking the rules, you don't want to help me have my fun, is that it?"

"No," Sarah said. "It's not like that at all." She was trying to figure out a way to make sense of what she was feeling, but she knew Balthazat was right. She should have told her mom and dad about the secret room as soon as she found it. She knew she shouldn't have played in it without getting permission first. Now she was trapped. If she did the right thing and didn't take Balthazat with her, he would be very upset. But if she did take him with her, she would be breaking another rule, and she knew that might mean even more trouble down the road.

"So what is it, then?" Balthazat asked.

Sarah looked down at him and knew at once that she simply could not pass up the chance to have a talking cat for a pet, no matter how many rules she had to break. She bent over and picked him up. "You're coming with me, of course," she said.

"Bravo," Balthazat said. "I knew you would make the right decision. Now, put me down, please." Sarah dropped him and he shook out his fur. "Shhh," he suddenly hissed, lifting his head as high as it would go. He sniffed at the air, the way he had when he'd first seen Sarah.

"What is it?" she asked.

"Shhh," he hissed again.

Sarah looked toward where he was sniffing and saw Lefty facing that way, too. A cool wind gusted through the trees, and as the shadow branches shifted, she saw a shape in the distance, white against the black, moving toward them.

"A sentinel," Balthazat whispered. He looked up at Sarah. "We need to hide you quickly."

"But where?" she asked.

"Lefty, down on the ground. Pretend you're asleep." Lefty did as he was told, dropping to his knees and rolling over so that his open palm faced the dark blue sky. "Now get in," Balthazat said to Sarah. "But be careful of his eye."

Sarah crawled onto Lefty's giant palm. He closed his eye and she curled around it. Then he closed his fingers into a loose fist, surrounding her except for a small space near his thumb. Balthazat poked his head in. "Everything will be fine as long as you stay quiet."

"I will," Sarah promised, and as Balthazat pulled his head back, she moved forward, pushing her face into the space, not only so she could breathe but so she could see what was happening, too.

The sentinel came down the path slowly, carrying something in his left hand. He looked like a normal man, Sarah thought, except for how pale his skin was. As he got closer, Sarah changed her mind. He wasn't normal after all. His chest and feet were bare and his pants were made of some rough black fabric held up by a length of dark brown rope knotted around his waist. His head was bald and his eyes and mouth were stitched shut with X's made of thick black thread. The object in his left hand was a head in a sling made of red rope. He carried it as if it were a lantern, holding it at arm's length in front of him. The head gave off no light, however. Its eyes and mouth were unstitched and open. Sarah wondered which one was the sentinel: the head in the sling or the body carrying it. For a moment, it looked like he was going to walk right past them, but then the head in the sling caught sight of Balthazat and the body changed direction. The cat ran ahead to meet him.

CHAPTER II

A Close Call

"Balthazat," the head in the sling said, "what are you doing out here?"

"Looking for you, actually."

"That so?"

"Yes."

"What for?"

"Jeb has finally gone off the deep end. He's locked me out of my cabin and won't let me in."

"What's wrong with Lefty?"

"I don't know. I think Jeb may have done something to him. He was trying to help me get back in. When I realized it was fruitless, we came looking for you. Then Lefty said he was tired and he just curled up like that."

"Maybe I should have a look at him," the sentinel said, and started toward Lefty. Sarah reflexively backed up and held her breath. She realized only now that her heart was pounding fiercely, drumming in her ears. It seemed so loud that she worried the sentinel might hear it.

"No, no, no," Balthazat said. "You must do something about Jeb first. I'll stay here with Lefty."

The sentinel stood still. After a moment, he said, "All right," then started up the path toward the clearing and the cabin.

Once he had vanished from sight, Lefty opened his fingers and Sarah crawled out of his palm. "Good work, Lefty," Balthazat said. "We must hurry now. They'll know I was lying in just a few minutes."

Lefty got back to his feet, and the three of them continued along the path until they reached the black mountain. Sarah found the spot where she had fallen, then pointed up. "I think I came out of that hole there."

Balthazat shook his head. "Of course you did," he said. He looked at Lefty. "Ironic, isn't it? All this time it was right in front of us." Lefty blinked at him.

"What was right in front of you?" Sarah asked.

"That hole you came through is called a breach. It's a crossover from here to there or from there to here, depending on which way you're going. There are supposed to be many of them all over Scotopia. I've been trying to find one for a very long time."

"But why?" Sarah asked.

"For the same reason that you think it's so much fun visiting here," Balthazat said. "I have always wanted to visit where you come from. That's why Lefty brought you to me and why I was so glad that he did. Because I hoped you could show me right to what I was searching for. And now you have. So let's hurry. We can't waste any more time. Pick me up, please."

Sarah did as she was told. Lefty stepped up behind her and used his thumb and index finger to pick both her and Balthazat up and lift them onto a small ledge just below the breach. Balthazat jumped from her arms, scrambling into the mouth of the hole. He faced Sarah.

"Can you make it?" he asked.

"I think so, but what about Lefty?"

"He can take care of himself. Come on now."

Sarah looked back at Lefty. She was sad to leave him behind. She was afraid of what would happen to him because of the lies Balthazat had told the sentinel. She realized then that it would probably be worse for Jeb, since Balthazat had said he had done something bad when he really hadn't. But what could she do about it? Lefty could never fit inside the breach, and even if he could, a giant hand with an eye in the center of its palm was not the kind of thing she could say she found in the bushes outside her house. She lifted her hand and waved at him. He waved back, then turned away from the mountain and started into the forest. Sarah turned around and pulled herself up.

It was very dark inside the hole, and she wished she had brought her flashlight. Then she remembered: she had. She quickly patted herself down, but the flashlight was gone. She moved to the edge of the hole and looked at the black sand below. She was almost sure she had dropped it when she had come through the first time. It was probably buried somewhere down there.

"What's wrong?" Balthazat hissed.

"I think my flashlight is down there."

"Never mind that. There's no time. Besides, you could never climb back up without Lefty. Come on. I can see well enough to guide us. Just hold on to my tail."

Sarah did as she was told.

The inside of the hole was as smooth as it was dark. They moved quickly and soon lost even the feeble light from Scotopia behind them. Sarah felt the tunnel angling upward, and then she saw faint yellow light ahead of them.

"That's it," she said. "That must be my room."

Balthazat continued climbing until they came to a wooden ledge. Sarah lifted Balthazat onto the floor beyond the ledge, then hoisted herself up. Sure enough, they were inside the secret room behind the bookcase. Sarah was greatly relieved. Balthazat, on the other hand, was so excited he darted right past the bookcase into her room without her. Sarah followed him quickly.

When she saw her room again, there was something strange about it, as strange as the Forest of Shadows had appeared to her when she'd first seen it. She looked around, trying to find anything familiar, but it all seemed different.

"I can't very well do this myself," Balthazat said, and Sarah saw that he was standing with his front paws on the middle shelf of the bookcase. She giggled, then used her feet to push the bookcase back into the wall. When she was sure it was all the way in, she got up and checked the edges with her fingers. Satisfied, she took off her slippers and flopped onto her bed. She hadn't realized how tired she was until now. "You can't go to sleep yet," Balthazat whispered.

"You need to open the window so I can get into the bushes in the morning and you can 'find' me."

Sarah gasped. "Oh, no!" she said.

"What is it now?" Balthazat asked.

"We're on the second floor."

Balthazat sighed. "Let's have a look."

Sarah unlatched the window over her bed and pushed it up. She and Balthazat peered into the darkness. The ground was too far away, she was sure.

"Oh," Balthazat said. "That's nothing."

"Really?"

"Not for the King of the Cats," he said, and sprang out. Sarah couldn't help letting out a little squeak of fear as she watched Balthazat sail through the dark, but he landed on the ground on all fours. He turned around, flicked his tail twice, then said, "See you in the morning," and darted into the bushes.

Her mouth still open in surprise, Sarah pulled her head back in, then closed the window and dropped her head to her pillow.

Before she knew it, she was asleep.

CHAPTER 12

Soul's Midnight

Sarah was in court, standing in front of a desk behind which was a huge four-armed man in a black robe and one of those white wigs that looked like carpet. "Guilty!" he shouted, and banged his gavel down on the desk. Sarah shook her head, confused. She didn't understand how she had gotten here, let alone what she was guilty of.

"But—" she said, and the judge cut her off by banging the gavel down again.

"Guilty!"

Sarah turned around, hoping to find someone who could help her. She was happy to see her parents and Billy sitting on a long bench. They were dressed in black clothes, as if they were going to a funeral. Her mother even had on one of those hats with a net that covered the face.

"Mom?" Sarah said.

When her mother tried to say something, the judge banged his gavel down a third time and shouted, "Guilty!"

Sarah faced him, frustrated and angry. "Stop banging that thing!" she yelled.

But the judge didn't stop. Instead, he banged the gavel down again and again and again.

Sarah reached up to plug her ears with both hands and nearly fell out of bed.

She wasn't in court at all; it had just been a dream. But where was she? One thing she knew for certain: she wasn't in her bedroom. If she had been, she would have been looking at the horse posters she had on the ceiling over her bed. But the ceiling here was white and full of cracks.

All at once she remembered she was in Grandma Winnie's house. And then the rest of it came to her: the trip to Scotopia, bringing Balthazat back, watching him hop out the window. Had that all been a dream, too, she wondered? But before she could answer her own question, the banging came again, louder than ever. It seemed to be coming from downstairs.

She looked at the clock. It was exactly 3:00 a.m. What could Mom and Dad be doing at this hour?

Throwing the covers back, Sarah got out of bed, turned on the light, and hurried to the door. She opened it a crack and peered into the hallway. She was glad to see that Billy's door was closed. He could sleep through anything, and she didn't feel like dealing with him right now.

"I'm telling you it's not the pipes," she heard her father say, his voice thick with sleep. "It's someone at the door."

"At this hour?" her mom replied. "They'll wake the children."

"I know," Dad said.

Too afraid to go back to bed, Sarah ran down the stairs as fast as she could. "What's going on?" she asked.

Mom and Dad looked at her. "Go back to bed," her mom said.

The banging sounded again, and this time they all faced the front door together.

Dad tied his robe closed angrily and stomped to the door. He tried to find the peephole, then realized there wasn't one. With a sigh, he tried to open the door, but it was locked. Sarah could tell that he was ready to let whoever was out there really have what he called a piece of his mind. This meant it was very likely Dad would be yelling soon.

The banging sounded again and Dad finally got the lock open and flung the door wide. Whatever he was going to say never made it past his lips.

There was no one there.

Dad looked at Mom and Sarah, his "I'm going to give you a piece of my mind" face completely gone. Then he turned toward the empty doorway again and pushed the squeaking screen open. He stepped out and looked around, but there was no one in sight.

"No one," Dad said.

Mom moved forward to see for herself. "Well," she said. "Maybe it was the pipes after all."

Dad grunted in agreement and closed the door. They started back to their room and Sarah said, "Wait."

"What is it, sweetie?" Dad asked.

Sarah was about to ask if she could sleep in their bed with them, but she suddenly realized she was only doing it out of habit. To her surprise, she wasn't really as afraid as she thought she ought to be. She saw her parents staring at her, waiting. "Good night," she said.

Mom and Dad traded glances.

"You okay to go back up by yourself?" Dad asked.

Sarah nodded and smiled. She really was okay to go back upstairs by herself. Maybe Dad was right after all. She had faced some pretty big fears on her trip to Scotopia and she wasn't nearly as afraid as she used to be.

"All right, then. Let's see you do it."

Sarah found the light switch and turned it on, then went upstairs without looking back.

As she headed toward her room, she glanced down the hall and was surprised to see Billy's door open and the light on. She walked over and looked in, but he wasn't in bed. Two worries flashed through her mind: first, that he was playing a practical joke and would jump out from some hiding place to scare the pajamas off her; second (and far worse), that he knew about the secret passage behind the bookcase in the yellow room and had gone through on his own.

As quickly as she could, Sarah turned on her heels and rushed to her room. She saw that the bookcase was still pushed into the wall. Billy was there, sitting on the floor, a big red book in his lap. But his chin was on his chest. He was asleep.

Sarah approached him and bent down to shake his shoulder gently. "Billy," she said. "What are you doing in here?"

"I heard someone knocking," he said.

"That was downstairs."

"No," he insisted. "It was in here. They were pounding this book on the floor."

Sarah frowned. "You were just dreaming," she said, and tried to take the book from his lap, but he held on to it with an iron grip.

"No," he said. "I want to keep it."

Anxious to get him out of her room as soon as possible, Sarah said, "Fine," and then got him to his feet and through the door. "Now go back to bed."

He waved at nothing and kept walking. Sarah waited until he was through the door of his room; then she climbed into bed and pulled the covers over her head.

CHAPTER 13

The Morning After

When Sarah woke, she jumped to her hands and knees, unlatched the window, and flung it open, peering outside. "Balthazat?" she called in as loud a whisper as she dared.

For a long moment, she heard only suburban silence: a car passing on the street, a dog barking, some kids yelling.

"Balthazat?" she called again, less certain this time. But then she saw him in the bushes below, looking up at her. He meowed loudly, and she got out of bed, put on her slippers, and ran downstairs.

As she streaked through the kitchen to the back door, Dad lowered his paper and said, "Hey, where do you think you're going?"

"Outside."

"Not while you're still in your pajamas."

"But Dad, I think I heard a cat out there. He sounded like he was in trouble."

Dad looked out the window into the backyard. "All right," he said. "But let me come with you."

"No," Sarah said. "I can do it."

"I know you can. With my help." Dad folded his paper and put it down. He took one more sip of coffee, then got to his feet and went outside with her.

Sarah hurried down the steps onto the grass and turned left. She stopped at the bushes in front of the fence and kissed the air as loudly as she could. "Here, kitty, kitty!" she called.

Balthazat answered with a loud meow and Dad stepped forward quickly. "Wait a second," he said as he pushed the bushes apart. "Let me pick it up. We don't know how friendly it is, and I don't want you to get scratched." He reached down carefully and grabbed Balthazat by the scruff of his neck. The cat froze so stiffly, Sarah thought he looked like a stuffed toy. Once Dad had Balthazat out of the bushes, he set him on the porch and patted his head. "I wonder who he belongs to."

"He doesn't have a collar," Sarah said, as if she had just noticed this. "So he must not belong to anybody."

"That's not necessarily true," Dad said. "Lots of people don't put collars on their cats."

"Why not?"

"Cats like to explore bushes and small places. The collar might get caught on something and the cat could be stuck."

"Do you think he belonged to Grandma?"

Dad shook his head. "I don't think so."

"Can we keep him?"

"No, honey. We have to find out if he belongs to someone."

"How?"

"After breakfast, we'll go around the neighborhood and ask people if they've seen him before. If nobody has, then we'll have to take him to the pound."

"No, Dad!" Sarah said. "We can't do that. We have to keep him!"

Dad sighed. "I guess we can see what your mother says."

"Deal," Sarah said, and smiled at Balthazat. "Shouldn't we feed him now? Maybe he's hungry."

Dad nodded. "I suppose. I think I saw a can of tuna in a cupboard somewhere."

Dad opened the back door and Balthazat shot through, into the kitchen. He stopped in the middle of the room, sat down, and began meowing loudly. Sarah and Dad both laughed. Moments later, Mom and Billy came downstairs.

"Do I hear a cat?" Mom asked.

Dad nodded. "Sarah found him outside."

"Can't we keep him, Mom?" Sarah asked. "Please?"

"I don't know if that's a good idea."

"Just while we're here."

Mom and Dad exchanged knowing glances. Perhaps they knew that when it was time to go back to California, Sarah would no doubt beg for the cat to come with them.

"I guess," Mom said.

Dad explained how they planned to ask around the neighborhood first, to see if the cat belonged to anyone. Mom agreed that was a good idea.

Billy came over and knelt down next to Sarah. "What's his name?" he asked.

"Balthazat," Sarah said without thinking. Balthazat looked at her and his eyes went wide.

Mom and Dad both laughed. "Baltha-who?" Dad asked.

"Balthazat," Sarah said again, quickly trying to think of an explanation for how she had picked such a strange name. "That's the name of a cat in a book I'm reading right now."

"Oh," they said, and Balthazat looked at her. She was sure he was smiling.

After breakfast, they did as Dad wanted and put Balthazat into a box to take him around the neighborhood. It was a complete waste of time, of course. Nobody was missing a cat, and nobody had seen Balthazat before.

"All right," Dad said after they had knocked on every door in a three-block radius. He looked at Sarah. "Looks like Balthazat has found a new home."

"Thanks, Dad," Sarah said, and gave him the biggest hug she could.

"Okay," he said. "You're welcome. But remember, you're responsible for him. Understand? Don't let him tear up any of Grandma's furniture before we can sell it."

Sarah nodded. "I think he'll be good."

"Oh?" Dad said. "Did I ever tell you about my cat, Lola?"

"Only about a hundred times," Sarah said.

"Then this will make a hundred and one," he said, and started telling Sarah the story of Lola, the cat he and Mom had had before Sarah and Billy were born, and how she used to rip up their curtains and furniture. In spite of how many times Sarah had heard the story, she laughed at the way her dad told it.

When they got home, Dad told Mom they needed to put cat food on the grocery list.

Sarah thanked them both again, then took Balthazat up to her room and closed the door. She could hardly wait to have a real conversation with him. Apparently, he felt the same way, because as soon as the latch clicked shut he said, "Well, that was humiliating."

"I'm sorry, Balthazat," Sarah said, dropping onto her

bed. "I had no idea it would all be so complicated. But it's over now."

"Good," he said, jumping up next to her. "Now we can get down to business."

"What do you mean?" Sarah asked.

Balthazat stepped closer to her, lowering his voice to a purring whisper. "What do you say we take a little trip?"

Sarah sat up straight. "You mean back to Scotopia?"

"No, no, no," Balthazat said. "To Penumbra. I've heard it's much more exciting than Scotopia."

"Really?" Sarah asked.

Balthazat nodded.

Sarah's shoulders sagged. "I'd love to," she said glumly. "But I don't think we can."

"Why not?" Balthazat asked, his tail getting bushy.

"For one thing, the door is locked."

"So we find the key."

Sarah hesitated. "That's not the only reason...," she said.

"Don't tell me you're having second thoughts again."

"I don't know," Sarah sighed. "I had a weird dream last night. It made me think about what you said. About how we weren't supposed to be going through to these places."

Balthazat stared at her for a long moment. Then he slowly shook his head and said, "I'm afraid I've had the wrong idea about you. After what we went through to escape the sentinel and then what we went through this morning, I thought you were a brave and clever girl."

Sarah bristled. "I am," she said.

"Not if you're going to let a little thing like this stand in your way. After all, you've already been through one door. I hardly see how going through another can be any worse."

Sarah thought about it for a minute, then shrugged. "I suppose we could try to find the key," she said.

Balthazat nodded slowly. "Now you're talking," he purred. "Where should we start?"

Sarah shrugged. "Grandma's desk, I guess. I need to pack it up anyway. Plus, when the boxes are full, that will give us an excuse to go down to the basement."

"Excellent thinking," Balthazat said, and together they went to the desk and started their search.

CHAPTER 14

The Key Is Found

Two hours later, Sarah had been through every drawer, every cubbyhole, every envelope, every metal box bound with rubber bands, every jar—all to no avail. She had filled three boxes with the contents of the desk but had not found the key.

Sarah was about to tell Balthazat she was ready to give up when the door flew open and Billy ran in. "Look what I found," he said. "It's the key to that door in the basement, I just know it." He held up his hand and when Sarah saw the key, she jumped to her feet and ran over to him.

"Let me see that," she said, and grabbed it from him.

"Hey!" Billy shouted. "Give it back. It's mine! I found it."

"Where did you find it?"

"None of your business." Billy jumped up to grab the key from Sarah's hand, but she held it out of his reach.

"Hold on a second," she said. "I just want to look at it."

Billy glared at Sarah and then suddenly turned and ran from the room. Glad to be rid of him, Sarah whirled around and bent down so Balthazat could see the key, too.

"What do you think?" he whispered.

Sarah nodded. It sure looked like it belonged to the lock in the basement. It was big and ornately carved with fine dark lines that looked almost like Egyptian hieroglyphs or Celtic runes. "Only one way to find out," she said.

When she stood up and turned around, Dad was standing in the doorway, his hand held in front of him, palm up.

Behind him stood Billy, arms folded across his chest, a satisfied smirk on his face. Sarah had never felt quite as angry as she did at that moment. She didn't know what to do, so she decided to play dumb.

"What?"

"You know exactly what!" Billy shouted. "Give me back my key."

Dad turned to Billy. "It's not your key, Billy. At least, not yet. If it fits that lock downstairs, I'll need to keep it. If it doesn't, then you can have it." Dad faced Sarah again. "So?"

Sarah hesitated. If the key fit the lock and her parents opened the door and discovered Penumbra, then it wouldn't be a secret anymore and everything that Balthazat had warned her about would actually happen. Everything would be ruined.

"Sarah?" Dad said, his voice getting sharper. "You do realize how much trouble you're already in, right?"

"For what?"

"You can't take things that don't belong to you."

"That's what he did."

"No!" Billy shouted. "I was taking it down to Mom and Dad."

"You're such a liar."

"Sarah!" Dad shouted, and he suddenly had that "I'm going to give you a piece of my mind" look on his face.

Realizing she had no choice, Sarah started to bring the key out from behind her back when Balthazat leaped through the air and scratched her arm. She shrieked in pain and dropped the key. It clattered to the floor and slid to a stop in front of Billy. But before he could bend over and pick it up, Balthazat hissed at him. Billy jumped away. Even Dad took a step backward. Then, like a dog, Balthazat picked the key up in his mouth and ran out of the room.

"What the—?" Dad said.

"Hey," Billy yelled, "come back here!" Then he ran after

the cat. Dad yelled at him to stop and then Sarah pushed past him and ran ahead. She reached the top of the stairs just in time to see Balthazat dash around the corner into the kitchen.

Then she heard Mom yell and something crash and the cat yowl.

When Sarah rounded the corner, she couldn't believe her eyes. Mom was on the floor, a whole drawer's worth of silverware scattered around her. In the middle of it, stuck to a fork, was the key. Balthazat, his tail as bushy as a bottle brush, was in the back corner. Sarah couldn't move. Not until Dad came down the stairs and pushed her aside as he hurried to help Mom to her feet. Billy came in next and dashed forward to grab the key. No sooner had he stood up straight than Dad snatched the key from his hand.

"Enough!" he shouted. "Billy, I want you to sit down at that table and don't move. Sarah, I want you to go upstairs and stay in your room until lunch."

"What?"

"Don't make it any worse than it already is."

"Come on, Balthazat," she said.

"No," Dad said. "You go to your room alone. And I am having serious second thoughts about keeping this cat here for even one more day."

"But Dad—" Sarah pleaded.

"That does it!" Dad said, shouting louder. "Now you can stay in your room until dinner."

Sarah stared at Balthazat, but he looked away. She looked at Billy, but he just stuck his tongue out at her. She opened her mouth to tell Dad what he had done, then decided she should quit while she was ahead. She didn't want to get in more trouble. She hung her head, then went up to her bedroom and closed the door.

She flopped onto her bed, and as she stared at the ceiling, it occurred to her how long it had been since she had been in trouble like this. She started to get angry. First with Billy because he was so annoying. Then with herself for taking the key and then talking back to her dad. If only she had waited, she probably could have traded Billy something for it and avoided the whole scene. Then she got mad at her dad for making her punishment so severe. Dinner was hours away! And then she realized she was even mad at Balthazat. This was really all his fault. Some friend he is, she thought. This simply wasn't fair.

And then, all at once, she realized it didn't matter. She didn't have to stay in her room if she didn't want to. Not when the door to Scotopia was right behind her bookcase. She sat up and smiled. "Yeah," she whispered. Once she was there, she could find Lefty. She was sure he could take care of her and hide her from the sentinels. Maybe she could even go to Balthazat's cabin and see if Jeb could take care of her—if he was still there. And if he wasn't, maybe she could take over the cabin. After all, without her help, Balthazat couldn't go home. So maybe she would just stay in Scotopia and never come back here at all.

Sarah nodded and got to her feet. After pulling the bookcase out of the wall, she slipped behind it. She started toward the hole, then stopped. If anyone came into her room now, they would see the bookcase open and Scotopia wouldn't be a secret anymore. Sarah went back and carefully pulled the bookcase into the wall behind her. Once she was sure it was tight, she went to the wooden ledge and jumped into the darkness.

CHAPTER 15

Back to Scotopia

Sarah was ready for the drop this time and managed to stay awake even as she fell onto the black sand and rolled over. She got to her hands and knees as fast as she could and peered through the forest, straining to spot any sign of a sentinel. The last thing she needed now was to be caught by one of them and sent on a one-way trip to see the King of Scotopia.

Once she was sure she was alone, she got to her feet, dusted off her hands, and started along the path. Without Lefty or Balthazat to guide her, however, she was unsure whether she was going in the right direction. Finally, she turned right and kept walking until she reached the edge of the silver stream. She was surprised at how far away from it she had gotten—and so quickly. She adjusted her path and continued walking.

At last, she emerged from the forest into the clearing,

although at a different place from where Lefty had originally brought her. She was farther to the right, facing the side of Balthazat's cabin instead of the front. She was eager to reach the cabin, but she was afraid that perhaps the sentinel was still there. She even considered the possibility that there might be more than one and that they had Jeb— and Lefty, too, perhaps—held against their will and were hurting them until they confessed what Balthazat had done. She crouched down as she neared the cabin, hoping to get close enough for a look through the side window before she went to the door.

Sure enough, she saw the sentinel and Lefty inside the cabin. To her surprise, however, the sentinel wasn't hurting Lefty. In fact, they were sitting in front of the fire together. Before she could figure out what was going on between them, the sentinel broke into a thunderous laugh, slapping Lefty on the back. Sarah was terribly confused. It looked to her like Lefty and the sentinel were friends. Maybe Lefty had tricked the sentinel into believing that Lefty was bad like him.

Sarah couldn't be sure of anything except that she had to stay clear of the sentinel. She decided she should go back across the clearing to hide in the forest and watch the cabin until the sentinel left. Maybe then she could find Jeb, or get Lefty to help her find him.

She moved carefully around the front of the cabin, then headed back into the shadow trees. A short way into the forest, she turned around and got down on the ground. She was in a perfect position to see the front door, and she was sure she could not be seen herself.

She hadn't been there for five minutes when she heard a cracking sound, like two rocks hitting each other. Reflexively, Sarah snapped her head to the left. She squinted through the trees and spotted a sliver of white moving behind them. The cracking sound came again, and Sarah decided she should get a closer look. After all, if it was another sentinel, she wanted to know so she could find a new hiding place.

She moved through the trees slowly. The cracking sound came more frequently. As she edged closer to the mysterious figure, she saw that it wasn't a sentinel—it was Jeb. He held a rock high over his head and brought it down on something at his feet. This was the cracking sound. She waited until she saw him lift the rock over his head again, then called out in a loud whisper, "Jeb."

Jeb was so startled he nearly dropped the rock on his own head. He whipped around and squinted at the trees. Sarah lifted her hand and stepped out.

"Hi," she said.

Jeb's face—the half he had, anyway—went limp and he

dropped the rock. "What are you doing here?" he said. "Did his plan work already?"

Sarah took another step forward. "So you *can* talk?"

"Of course I can talk," Jeb said, and turned away, as if suddenly remembering what he looked like. "I'm just not the kind of thing you want to look at for too long."

"That's not true," Sarah said. "Besides, if you don't let people look at you, how do you expect to look at them?"

Jeb faced her slowly. "You didn't answer my question: did his plan work already?"

"Whose plan?"

"Balthazat's. The King of the Cats. That's what he told you he was, right?"

Sarah frowned. "Yes," she said. "Isn't that what he is?"

Jeb shook his head. "No. He lied to you."

"What?" Sarah said, more confused than ever.

"Everything he told you was a lie."

Sarah wasn't sure if she should smile or frown. "What do you mean everything he told me was a lie?"

"Exactly that. For starters, he's not the King of the Cats."

"Then who is he?"

"The King of Scotopia."

"Don't be silly," Sarah said. She was starting to get angry. Balthazat had told her the King of Scotopia was bad. "He said nobody knows who the King of Scotopia is."

"I know," Jeb said. "He told me the same thing when I first got here."

"Why would he do such a thing?"

"Because he's been trying to find a way over for a very long time."

"A way over?"

"To where we come from. I came through just like you did, two years ago. I found a secret passage in my aunt's house and I went through it. When I got here, I wandered all over until I was caught by a sentinel, who took me to Balthazat. He told me he was the King of the Cats. All the same things he told you. He told me he wanted to come back with me and be my pet. The problem was, I couldn't remember where I had come through, and no matter how much we looked, we couldn't find it. Balthazat got very angry with me. He stopped pretending to be a cat and showed me what he really looks like. Then he took half my face and told me that I could have it back if we ever found a way over."

Sarah was stunned. "But he said you lost your face in a bet with the blemmyes."

"Another lie."

"But why would he take your face?"

"To keep me here. He knows I can't go back home with only half a face. Nobody would be able to look at me."

"Stop saying that. I don't have a problem looking at you."

Jeb smiled slightly. It seemed to Sarah like he hadn't smiled in a very long time. "Okay, so maybe you'd be nice, but I know the truth about other people. They would laugh at me and send me away to live someplace where no one would have to see me." He bent over and picked up a glass box at his feet. He held it out to Sarah and she gasped when she saw the missing half of his face inside. "See? This is where he keeps it. In this box. I took it from where he hides it in the cabin. But I can't get it open, no matter what I do. And I can't break the glass, either. I'm sure he's the only one who can open it. Besides, even if I could get it open, I'm not sure I could put my face back on."

Sarah frowned. "You said something about Balthazat having some kind of plan."

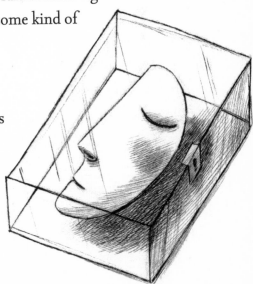

Jeb nodded.

"A plan for what?"

"To steal the sleepers and bring their souls back here so that the darkness can never be complete."

"Sleepers?"

Jeb nodded. "People who die aren't really dead, exactly. Their souls just go to sleep. And at the end of time, the souls of all the people who did bad things and never said they were sorry will come here, to Scotopia, where shadows and darkness come from. The darkness of their souls will make Scotopia completely dark. The souls of all the people who did good things without expecting reward will go to Ormaz, the place where light comes from. In Ormaz, they will shine like bright candles forever. Balthazat knows he can't tell which sleepers are dark souls and which ones are light, but he figures if he takes a bunch, he ought to end up with a few lights and then it will never be completely dark here."

Sarah began to feel sick to her stomach. "What's the place called? Where the dead go to sleep?"

"Penumbra," Jeb said.

Sarah felt even sicker. "Balthazat told me that Penumbra had nothing to do with that."

Jeb laughed bitterly. "Of course he did. I told you: everything he says is a lie."

"So Penumbra really is where the dead go to sleep?"

Jeb nodded grimly. "The house you're staying in is like a train station, the place where the dead come after they're dead but before they go to Penumbra."

"How do you know so much about it?"

"My aunt was what is called a record keeper. I think she had plans for me to take over when it was her turn to go to Penumbra. But then I came here and forgot how to get back."

"Oh, no," Sarah said, and started to cry.

CHAPTER 16

A New Friendship

Jeb rushed toward her and put his hands on her shoulders. "What's wrong?" he asked.

Sarah wiped her eyes. "This is what you wanted to tell me yesterday, before we left, isn't it?"

Jeb nodded. "Of course I wanted to warn you. But I knew I couldn't, not if I ever hoped to see my face again or have any chance of getting back home."

Sarah wiped the tears from her face. "I had no idea."

"But why are you crying?"

In detail, Sarah explained how Balthazat had talked her into going to Penumbra. How she knew where the door was. How her brother had found a key but she had been sent to her room before they had tried it.

"Did he have the journal, too?" Jeb asked.

"What journal?"

"The record keepers each have a journal. The names

of the dead appear in this book when it is their time to go into Penumbra. When the dead arrive at the house, the record keeper checks their name off and then uses the key to open the door to Penumbra. But they must be used together."

Sarah blinked and sniffed. "What do you mean?"

"The key won't work without the journal and the journal won't work without the key. I don't know exactly how or why. But from what I understand, the only way you can see the dead when they arrive is if you're holding the journal. That's the only way the key works, too."

Sarah stopped crying. Maybe it wasn't as hopeless as she had thought. "Does Balthazat know any of this?"

Jeb shrugged. "If he does, he didn't hear it from me. He kept asking me what I knew about Penumbra, but I always told him I didn't know anything."

Sarah nodded. "Well, good on that," she said.

Jeb laughed. "So your brother didn't have the journal?"

"Maybe," Sarah said. She explained how she had found Billy in her room with a big red book in his lap. She suspected that it might be the journal and that that was where he had found the key.

Jeb nodded. "But if he doesn't know they need to be used together..."

"Exactly," Sarah said. "That means we might still have

time to stop him." Now it was her turn to grab Jeb by the shoulders. "You have to come with me."

Jeb pulled away from her and shook his head. "I told you: I can't. I can't go back looking like this."

"You have to. I can't do this alone."

Thunderous laughter echoed across the clearing, and they both crept to the edge of the forest. The door to the cabin was open and Lefty and the sentinel were standing on the porch.

"So the sentinels really work for Balthazat?" Sarah whispered.

Jeb nodded. "That's right. Until you came through, they were searching for the way over."

"What about Lefty?"

"Him too. I think he was once like me."

"What do you mean?"

"I think he was someone who found a way here and couldn't show Balthazat the way back, so Balthazat changed him."

Sarah shook her head, worried about what Balthazat might do to her if he found out she knew the truth about him.

"That whole routine where Lefty hid you from the sentinel was just a trick to make you think he saved you from something bad."

"You know about that?"

"I told you: everything he did to you he did to me first."

"Except show me what he really looks like," Sarah said.

"You can be thankful for that," Jeb said.

"I am," Sarah said. "And I'm thankful I came back here and found you." She looked in Jeb's eye. "You've saved me, you know. Do you understand?"

Jeb smiled for the second time and nodded. "Yes."

Sarah smiled back. "Good," she said. "Then you'll do it? Come with me and help me finish what I've started? Help me set things right?"

Jeb nodded.

They looked back toward the cabin, where the sentinel and Lefty still stood on the porch.

"Come on," she whispered to Jeb, "we better get moving. There's no telling how long they'll stay there." Sarah got up and started back through the forest toward the black mountain.

Only when they reached the breach did Sarah remember that they couldn't get up without Lefty's help. She looked at Jeb.

"What do we do now?" she said.

"Here," Jeb said, locking his fingers together to give her a boost.

"But then you can't come with me."

"We don't really have a choice, do we? Now hurry. Before the sentinel or Lefty finds us."

Sarah threw her arms around Jeb and hugged him tightly. "I'll stop Balthazat and I'll make him give you back your face. I promise."

"Hurry up," Jeb said, and pulled out of Sarah's hug. She lifted her foot and put it into his hands. He boosted her up high, but her fingers still couldn't reach the ledge.

"Not high enough," she said.

"Hold on," he said, and grabbed her legs, pushing them up until he could get one foot in each hand. He pushed her up higher and higher. Her fingers stretched out farther and farther until she finally got hold of the ledge and pulled herself up. She sighed and collapsed onto the ledge, then looked back down into the forest. Her smile disappeared when she saw Lefty and the sentinel coming through the forest toward the mountain.

"Hurry, Jeb," she whispered. "They're coming. Run."

Jeb waved and took off as fast as he could, his feet kicking up black sand as he zigzagged through the trees. Sarah started to climb into the hole, but then noticed that Jeb had left his face behind. The glass box was on the sand near the trunk of a tree. She looked up. Jeb was so far away now that she would have to yell for him to hear her. But if she yelled, Lefty and the sentinel would hear her. She knew she couldn't let Jeb lose his face forever, so without thinking about it another moment, she jumped down from the ledge.

CHAPTER 17

Balthazat Tries Again

Billy was feeling especially pleased with himself. Not only did he have something that Sarah wanted—the key—but she had gotten in big trouble and he hadn't. He knew he wasn't supposed to be happy when people got in trouble, but Sarah didn't count. She was so mean to him all the time, and Mom and Dad hardly ever noticed. She really deserved to get punished more than she did.

Now he was in the basement with his parents, watching as Dad put the key in the big lock on the door. When it slid right in, Dad looked at Mom and smiled. "Wouldn't that be something?" he said, and turned the key.

But nothing happened. It just spun around and around. Dad took the key out.

"Oh, well," he said. "It was worth a try."

Mom nodded.

"So now I can have it?" Billy asked.

"If it's okay with your mother," Dad said.

Mom nodded, took the key from Dad and faced Billy. "Want me to tie it on a string for you? Then you can wear it around your neck."

Billy nodded and they all started upstairs.

"Why don't you call a locksmith?" Mom suggested.

"Bolt cutters will be a heck of a lot cheaper."

"Just seems a shame to cut that big old lock."

Dad shrugged as they went into the kitchen. "Where's the phone book? I need to find a hardware store."

Billy perked up. He liked the hardware store. There were all kinds of neat things to look at. "Can I go with you?" he asked.

"If Mom doesn't need you here."

"That's fine," Mom said. "But I need a few things, too." She found some string and tied the key to it. Then she put it around Billy's neck. He couldn't wait for Sarah to see it. Imagining her reaction made him smile.

Dad came in from the front room with the phone book in his hand. "Do you have a list?"

"Right here," Mom said. She picked a slip of paper up from the counter and gave it to him.

Dad glanced over it quickly. "All right." He turned to Billy. "Just give me a few minutes to see if Grandma had any of this stuff in the garage and then we'll go. Okay, partner?"

Billy nodded and they went outside. Dad headed to the garage and hoisted the door while Billy walked to the hammock and jumped in. As he swung back and forth, he picked up the key and held it between his fingers, staring at it. It really was cool. So dark and old, with tiny little scratches that Mom had said was called "engraving" on it in a knotted design.

"I wonder what it goes to?" Billy whispered to himself.

And then he heard a voice say: "The door in the basement."

Billy blinked and looked around. Through the back window, he could see his mom in the kitchen, taking things down from the shelves. So he said, "Dad?"

Dad poked his head around the side of the garage. "Yeah?"

"Did you say something?"

Dad shook his head.

"Oh," Billy said, and Dad went back into the garage.

"Not your dad," the voice whispered again. "Me."

Billy sat up and looked around again, but he couldn't see anyone.

"Down here," the voice whispered, and Billy looked at the row of bushes behind the hammock. All he could see was Balthazat poking his head through.

"Balthazat?" he said.

"Shhh," the cat said. "Please try to keep calm."

Billy gulped. "But you're a cat."

"More than that," said Balthazat. "I am the King of the Cats."

"But cats can't talk."

"Obviously we can."

"Mom!" Billy yelled in his loudest "I just fell off my bike and I think I broke my arm" voice.

"No, no, no," Balthazat said. "You can't let anyone else know that I can talk. Not even your sister. This has to be our secret."

Billy stared at Balthazat and suddenly smiled. He could think of nothing as sweet as having a secret from his sister—especially when that secret was a talking cat. Now he was sorry he had yelled like that.

The back door opened and Mom came out. "What is it, honey? What's wrong?" she called to him.

Billy looked at her. "Nothing."

"What do you mean 'nothing'? You sounded like you really hurt yourself or something."

Dad came out of the garage with a tape measure in his hand. "I'll say."

"Tell her you thought you saw a big spider," Balthazat whispered. "But everything's okay now."

"I thought I saw a big spider," Billy said. "But everything's okay now."

"Oh," Mom said, and went back inside. Dad went with her.

Billy climbed out of the hammock and got to his knees.

"Well," Balthazat said, "that was easy, wasn't it?"

Billy nodded. "So where did you come from?"

"A place called Penumbra," Balthazat said.

Billy's eyes went wide. "So it's real? The place behind the door in the basement?"

"Of course it's real. And it's supposed to be a secret. But the thing is, I need to get back there right away and I need your help."

"Really? Nobody ever needs my help."

"I guess you can't say that anymore."

Billy sucked in a breath. "I guess not," he said. "What do you need me to do?"

"I need you to use that key to open the door in the basement."

"We tried it already. It didn't work."

"That's because you weren't doing it correctly," Balthazat said.

Billy frowned. "Really? How are we supposed to do it?"

"Come upstairs with me and I'll show you."

"But I told my dad I'd go to the hardware store with him."

"You'd rather do that than hang out with the King of the Cats?"

Billy shrugged. "I guess not."

"Tell him you've changed your mind."

Billy nodded just as the back door opened and Dad came out. "You ready to go?" he called across the yard.

Billy looked at Dad, then at Balthazat, then back at his dad again. "No," he said. "I changed my mind."

"You sure?"

Billy nodded.

"Okay," Dad said. "Suit yourself."

Billy waited until Dad was in the van and backing out of the driveway before he turned to Balthazat and said, "What now?"

CHAPTER 18

A New Plan

Sarah hit the sand hard and rolled. Snatching up the glass box, she took off through the trees in the direction Jeb had run. She heard the sentinel and Lefty at her back, but when she looked over her shoulder, they were heading away from her. She turned around again and ran faster and faster until she was so out of breath that she collapsed to the ground and flopped onto her back.

Jeb peeked out from behind a tree. When he saw Sarah, he stepped out. "What are you doing?" he said. "You scared me half to death. I thought you were them."

"I'm sorry," Sarah said, and sat up. "But you forgot this." She showed him the glass case.

"Oh," he said, coming forward. He knelt next to her and took the case from her hands. "I don't know what to say. If they had found it, I would have never gotten it back." Jeb looked at her. "But what'll we do now? How will you get back?"

"We'll wait until they leave and you can boost me up again."

"What if they don't leave?"

"Oh," Sarah said. She hadn't considered that possibility. "Do you think we can find another way through?"

"Are you kidding? Balthazat and the sentinels never have."

"What about the one you came through? Couldn't we find that one?"

Jeb shrugged. "Maybe."

"We have to try," Sarah said. "Come on."

They walked for a long time without talking, up and down hills of black sand in front of endless sections of black mountains. The farther they walked, the thinner Sarah's hope became. Every shadow tree they passed seemed to hover overhead like another bad thing about to happen. Sarah began to worry that maybe Balthazat did know about the journal and that he would trick Billy the way he had tricked her. She worried that Billy would open the door to Penumbra for him. That Balthazat would steal the sleepers and bring them back to Scotopia. That Jeb would never get his face put back together. She soon realized that thinking about all those bad things was only making her feel worse, so she decided to focus instead on what she could do to stop them. "Does any of this look familiar?" she asked.

"You're kidding, right?"

"I wasn't, really. But I'm beginning to understand how you couldn't find your way back to where you came through." The landscape was so similar to everything else she had seen so far that it seemed they had merely been walking in place. "Is all of Scotopia like this?"

"No. I've heard Balthazat talk about different places. He's had meetings, too, with the things in charge of those places."

"What do you mean?"

"One time, this disgusting thing named Hashmed came from a place called the Green Desert to report on a rebellion of the blemmyes. They wanted to get rid of Balthazat and take over Scotopia and try to make things better for everyone. But Balthazat stopped them before they even got started." Jeb shook his head.

Sarah looked around again. "It seems so obvious to me now that this is a bad place, full of bad things. I wonder how come I didn't see that when I first got here."

Jeb smiled. "If it makes you feel any better, I used to spend a lot of time asking myself that same question. But then I realized that I couldn't blame myself for not seeing the truth. And neither should you. We only did what any normal person would do. We believed the best about where we were and about those we met. Tell you the truth, I'd rather be that way and live with the mistakes than always think the worst of everything and everyone."

"Yeah," Sarah said. "Me too."

They walked in silence again for another stretch. When they came to a giant river, Sarah sat down on a black rock poking through the sand and put her chin in her hands. "Okay," she said. "I give up."

"You don't really mean that," Jeb said. "Do you?"

"We'll never find another way through. This place is huge, and it all looks the same. I doubt we'll even be able to find our way back to the one I came through. Besides, even if we could, it's probably too late. Balthazat may have figured out how to open the door to Penumbra by now."

"But we don't know that for sure," Jeb said, and knelt in front of Sarah. "Do you know how many times I've thought about giving up? How many times I decided that I would just quit trying? Trying to open this box. Trying to figure out a way back. Trying to stop Balthazat from his search. But every time I decided I would give up, I felt something give me a poke and remind me that there was still a chance. As long as we keep trying, there's always a chance. When I saw you come through the door of Balthazat's cabin, I knew that I had been right to not give up. So you can't give up. Because if you do, then all my hope will have been for nothing."

Sarah looked at him. She didn't feel so sad and tired anymore. "So what do we do if we can't find a way through?"

"I've been thinking about that," Jeb said. "Do you remember what I told you about the blemmyes?"

"From the Green Desert? The ones who wanted to start the rebellion?"

Jeb nodded and got to his feet. "I was thinking that if we could find them, maybe we could convince them to try again. We could tell them that Balthazat isn't here, so they have a real chance this time."

"That's a great idea!"

Jeb nodded. "We could get them to chase off Lefty and the sentinels, for one thing. And if you go back and find out Balthazat has already started his plan, then I'll be here waiting with the blemmyes to stop him from finishing it."

Sarah slapped her knees and stood up. "So do you have any idea how we get to the Green Desert?"

"Sure," Jeb said. "All we have to do is..." He stopped talking, but his mouth stayed open and then his eye went blank. It seemed to Sarah that he wasn't looking at her anymore, but behind her.

"Jeb?" she said. "What's wrong?"

"I forgot."

"Forgot what?"

He lifted his finger and pointed. "About him."

CHAPTER 19

Meet Mr. Ink

Sarah slowly turned around. For a long moment, she couldn't make sense of what she was seeing. The ground itself seemed to be lifting up in front of her, like a wave. Only it wasn't sand, it was darkness, thick and black. She saw dozens of hands stretching out from the edges of the black and then she saw eyes, hundreds of them, blacker even than the darkness that surrounded them. She felt something at her feet, and when she looked down, she realized she and Jeb were standing on whatever this thing was and it was now lifting the part they stood on, tipping them backward. She slammed into Jeb and he slipped back.

"What is it?" she shouted.

"His name is Mr. Ink," Jeb said. "He works for Balthazat, too."

"Of course he does," Sarah shouted. Then, for a brief

moment, she thought they might escape if they could just get off of Mr. Ink, but the other side, unseen until now, lifted up behind them and they fell, rolling together like balls in a sheet as the top closed overhead. The darkness inside was cold and complete.

"Jeb?" Sarah said. But he didn't answer. She reached out, patting her way through the black until she found him. She felt his arms and shoulders and face. "Jeb?" she said again, but it was clear that he had passed out.

Suddenly, she heard flapping sounds, like the wings of a hundred birds at once, and she knew they were flying somehow. Reflexively, she reached out to grab something to steady herself, but only succeeded in slipping farther down, in a different direction. She patted her hands along the smooth dark surface that surrounded her but didn't like the cold leathery feel of it. She had hoped to find an opening that she could look through, but now she would just have to wait and see where they went.

It wasn't long before Jeb came to, and Sarah explained to him what had happened. "And," she concluded, "I have no idea where we're going."

"I do," Jeb said. "That's what worries me."

"Where?" Sarah asked.

"You don't want to know."

"Tell me."

Jeb was silent for a long time before he finally said, "The Black Iron Prison."

At that very moment, the flying darkness that had them in its grip began its descent. The drop was so fast that Sarah yelped as her tummy fluttered. "The what?" she asked, trying to catch her breath.

"The Black Iron Prison," Jeb repeated. "It's where Balthazat puts anyone who doesn't agree with him."

"What happens to them?"

"Nothing. He just never lets them out."

"Oh," Sarah said, and her stomach fluttered again as their descent grew even more rapid. She wanted to ask him how Mr. Ink had found them, but then she realized it really didn't matter. And then they landed so suddenly that they both fell over.

Almost immediately, a seam of light opened overhead and the darkness peeled away. They had landed on a platform made of dark metal. Sarah wondered if it was iron and hoped it wasn't. She looked at Jeb, but he was staring straight ahead, at a row of six squat creatures standing in front of the platform, each holding a flickering torch of blue fire.

"Mr. Ink," one of the squat creatures said as it stepped

onto the platform. "Back from patrol, are you? And what have you brought for us this time?" The creature was close enough now that Sarah could see it had only one eye in the center of its forehead. She was starting to get to her feet, when a cold hand grabbed her upper arm, pulled her roughly to one side, and shoved her onto the platform. A moment later, Jeb crashed down next to her. When she looked over her shoulder, she saw the darkness shrinking into itself, taking the form of a tall man in a top hat and cape. He remained completely black, however, like a silhouette, or a pool of the stuff he was apparently named after.

"I found these two in the Forest of Shadows," Mr. Ink said. His voice sounded like wind from a cave. Sarah could feel it blowing across the back of her neck, lifting goose bumps. "They were on their way to the Green Desert to see the blemmyes."

Sarah felt her hope dwindle, like a candle flame sputtering. She hoped that Mr. Ink hadn't heard their whole plan.

"Is that a fact?" the cyclops said, pacing back and forth in front of Sarah and Jeb. "What for?"

"They said something about getting the blemmyes to start the rebellion again. Said something about Balthazat not being here."

The already dim hope inside Sarah went out completely.

The cyclops stepped closer and bent forward to get a closer look. "But isn't this Balthazat's houseboy?" he said as he lowered the torch toward Jeb's face. "Well?" the cyclops asked. "Aren't you?"

Jeb looked at him for a long moment, and Sarah saw something in his face that she had not seen before. It was anger, pure and simple. The intensity of it frightened her, and she got scared that he might do something that would make their situation worse. Before she could say anything, Jeb spit in the guard's eye. The cyclops reeled back and stood up straight. He held still for a long moment, then used the back of his arm to wipe his eye, slowly. He stepped toward Jeb, lowering the torch and pushing the burning end into Jeb's shoulder. Jeb screamed and jumped back. The cyclops moved forward to do it again, but Sarah, overcome with anger herself, grabbed the torch without thinking.

The cyclops faced her, and in one swift motion pulled the torch from her hand. He was much stronger than she was. When he pressed the burning end against her arm, she, too, shouted in pain. But not because the fire was hot—it was like ice, colder than anything she had ever felt. When he took the torch away, she rubbed the spot where it had been, trying to soothe the pain.

"This one, on the other hand," the cyclops said, "is definitely not from around here. Are you?"

Sarah looked at the cyclops, feeling sick. When she looked at Jeb, he shook his head, and she knew he meant for her to say nothing.

"So that's how it's going to be, huh?" the cyclops said. "All right. Take them away. Put them in the Blue Suite. I'll make them talk later. After dinner, perhaps."

Mr. Ink moved forward. A half-dozen hands suddenly shot from his middle. The hands grabbed Sarah and Jeb and hoisted them both to their feet. "Mind if I stick around and watch?" Mr. Ink asked.

"Not at all," the cyclops said as the other guards moved forward to take Sarah and Jeb, dragging them toward a door in the floor.

CHAPTER 20

In the Blue Suite

Sarah was scared now. And the deeper they took her and Jeb into the Black Iron Prison, the more scared she got. The rocklike confidence she had felt not so long ago turned to dust with every step toward the Blue Suite. She remembered now how she had been so angry with her mom and dad that she'd considered staying in Scotopia forever. That was beginning to sound like the silliest idea she'd ever had.

After being marched around countless corners and down endless flights of stairs, they reached a spiral stair-case and descended to a narrow walkway over a dark pit that seemed to fall away forever. Their one-eyed escorts pushed them toward a door. One of them took a key from a hook on the wall and unlocked it. They pushed Sarah and Jeb inside and slammed the door shut behind them.

The Blue Suite wasn't what Sarah had expected. First of

all, it wasn't a suite, it was simply a big rectangle of concrete painted blue and made bluer by the ranks of cold-fire torches that burned in fixtures set at intervals near the tops of the walls. Most of the smoke escaped through holes in the ceiling, but some of it filled the room like thin fog. As she scanned the room, Sarah saw that Jeb was crying.

"What's wrong?" she asked.

"This is all my fault," he said.

"No, it's not," Sarah told him.

"But it is," he insisted. "None of this would have happened if I hadn't dropped my face."

Sarah felt bad for Jeb. She didn't like to see anyone cry, especially not her friends. And she had definitely begun to think of Jeb as a real friend. Wanting nothing more than to make him feel better, she said, "That's not true."

Jeb sniffed. "What are you talking about?" he asked, his voice stiff with disbelief.

Sarah twisted her hair, trying to think of what to say next. And then she realized that it wasn't his fault—it was hers. "None of this would have happened if I hadn't jumped down to get your face for you. So if you want to know the truth, this is really my fault. But that still doesn't get us out of here."

Jeb sniffed again and wiped his eye. He began to smile as he understood what she was saying. "You're right. I guess it doesn't really matter whose fault it is, we need to find a way out."

"Hear, hear," a voice called from the darkness, and Sarah and Jeb both jumped and faced forward.

"Who's there?" Sarah said, fear returning to her chest like a bird to its nest.

A black shape formed in the thin smoke, and for a terrible moment, Sarah thought Mr. Ink had somehow joined them in the Blue Suite. Without really thinking, Sarah grabbed Jeb's hand just as a man stepped out of the shadows. Sarah was only slightly relieved to see that it was not Mr. Ink. This man was dressed in old-fashioned clothes, like an actor from a movie with cowboys in it. His pants were dark gray and his jacket had thin stripes and two long parts that hung off the back like tails. His shirt had frills at the cuffs and under his neck. His hair was black and slicked back and he had a mustache that looked like handlebars on a bicycle. "My name is Edgar," he said. "Edgar Merton. Born in New York City. Presently of San Francisco. How about you two?"

Sarah suddenly realized she was holding Jeb's hand and quickly let go of it. She hoped he hadn't noticed. When she looked at him, she saw that he wasn't paying attention to her at all. He was staring at Edgar.

"You're Edgar?" Jeb said. Edgar nodded. "The Edgar?"

Edgar laughed. "If by that you mean am I the only Edgar in this place, then I would have to answer in the affirmative."

Jeb smiled at Sarah. "This is Edgar. The Edgar."

Sarah frowned. She could tell Jeb was very excited, but she had no idea why. "I don't get it," she said.

"I've heard Balthazat talk about him."

"You have?" Edgar asked, surprised.

Jeb nodded. "He threatened me once. Said he would put me in the Blue Suite, just like he'd done with you."

Edgar smiled crookedly. "And here I thought he'd forgotten all about me."

"You're like us, right? You came over from the other side. A long time ago. Long before me." Jeb faced Sarah. "Just look at him. What year was it when you came over?"

"It was 1883," Edgar said.

Now it was Sarah's turn to express disbelief. "In 1883?" she said, frowning. "But how can that be? You shouldn't still be alive."

"Normally, that would be true," Edgar said. "However, before I became a—how shall I say—more permanent resident here, I had the opportunity to go back and forth several times. I discovered that as long as you are here, time stands still for you back on the other side. When I went back, it was as if I had only just stepped through."

Sarah thought about this for a long time. If what Edgar said was true, then things weren't really as bad as she had imagined. She looked at Jeb and they both smiled. Obviously he was reaching the same conclusion. "So it really isn't too late," she said. "Because it's still right before lunch back in my room. And it will be as long as I stay here."

"There is one exception, however," Edgar said.

"What is it?" Sarah asked.

"It's just a theory, but I think this only works when you go back through exactly the same way you came."

"That makes sense," Jeb said. "Your tunnel would lead back to 1883 and Sarah's would lead back to her present."

Edgar nodded.

"Wait a second," Sarah said, now remembering all the stuff about cause and effect from science class. "If my coming over here means time has stopped back there, what if something from here went back over there with me?"

Edgar's face darkened. "That's what Balthazat has been trying to do for a very long time," he said. "That's why I'm here, in fact. Because I refused to show him where I came through."

Jeb's half-mouth opened wide. "You mean you actually remember where you came through?"

"Of course. I spent a good deal of time mapping Scotopia before one of the sentinels caught me and brought me to Balthazat." Edgar's eyes grew distant, as if he was looking not at Sarah or Jeb or the walls around them but into his own memories. "He was so sweet at first. Telling me how he was the King of the Cats. Giving me good food to eat and that nice warm fire to sit by in his cozy cabin."

Sarah didn't feel so bad now. Yes, Balthazat had tricked her and Jeb. But he had tricked Edgar as well, and Edgar seemed like a very smart man.

Edgar's eyes grew still more distant as he continued remembering. "It didn't take me long to start seeing stars." He waved his hand through the air in front of him as though drawing a giant banner. "'Edgar and his Amazing Talking Cat!'" He faced Sarah and Jeb. "I told Balthazat that what he had here was nothing compared with what he could have back where I was from. He would be a star like nothing the world had ever seen. He refused at first, telling me he wasn't allowed to leave here because of his duties and so forth. But I persisted, working as hard as I could to convince him to come back with me." Edgar lowered his head grimly. "Ha! How terribly ironic it all seems now."

"I don't understand," Sarah said. "If Balthazat wanted to go back with you, why would he refuse?"

Edgar shook his head, as if shaking off all the memories that were crashing in on him. "To trick me, of course. To make me think it was my idea to take him back. To throw me off the scent of what he was really up to." Edgar sighed. "And it would have worked except that I saw his true form just before we left."

Jeb gasped and his eyes went wide. Edgar noticed and smiled sadly.

"You've seen it, too?"

Jeb nodded.

"I panicked when I saw it," Edgar said. "He wasn't a cat at all. He was a monster. And I knew then that it was all a trick. All a lie. That he was using me to find a way through to the other side. By then it was too late for me to turn back. If I did, he would have known I knew the truth. So I pretended I hadn't seen his real face. And then I pretended to forget where I had come through. After we returned to his cabin, I sneaked out, hoping I could escape and never return. But he was watching. The sentinels caught me. They took me back to Balthazat and he demanded that I tell him the way through. Then one of the sentinels found the map I had made. I barely managed to get it away from him before he could give it to Balthazat."

"What did you do with it?"

"I ate it," Edgar said, laughing. "It was the only way I could be sure that he couldn't get it. After that, he brought me here and said he would let me go only if I re-created the map for him."

Sarah and Jeb looked at each other. Neither one of them knew what to say. Finally, Sarah turned back to Edgar. "You still haven't answered my question."

"You mean about whether or not time stops if something went back over with you?" Edgar said. Sarah nodded sheepishly. "Is this a hypothetical question?"

"What does that mean?" she asked.

"Hypothetical means it hasn't happened yet."

"Oh," Sarah said. "Then I'm afraid this isn't a hypothetical question. Balthazat tricked me. I never saw his true form. I took him to the other side."

"Oh, dear," Edgar said. "But then you came back?"

Sarah nodded.

"Oh, double dear. I don't know what that does to my time theory."

"What do you mean?"

"Just that, I'm afraid. I don't really know. I would guess that with each of you where you aren't supposed to be, time would continue normally on both sides."

"Which means it is too late," Sarah said, and suddenly sagged. It was worse than she wanted to admit. Worst of all, this was more her fault than she had imagined. Not just because she had jumped down to save Jeb's face for him, but because she had come to Scotopia in the first place.

"Maybe . . . ," Jeb said. "But maybe Balthazat hasn't gotten to your brother yet. Maybe they don't even know about the journal."

"The journal?" Edgar said.

Jeb explained quickly how the journal and the key needed to be used together in order to open the door to Penumbra. He also explained how he had not revealed any of this to Balthazat.

"Then I have some bad news for you," Edgar said.

Sarah's heart sank still deeper. "You told him?"

Edgar nodded. "Long ago. Before I'd seen his true form, of course. My sister was a record keeper."

"So Balthazat will be able to get the door open," Sarah said. She faced Jeb. "And since we'll never get out of here, it's all hopeless."

CHAPTER 21

Some Very Bad News

E dgar clucked his tongue. "Now, now," he said. "It's not hopeless at all."

Sarah lifted her head slowly. "You don't know my brother."

"That's not what I'm talking about," Edgar said. "I'm talking about you getting us out of here."

Sarah pointed at herself and raised her eyebrows. Edgar nodded.

"How do you figure?" she asked.

Edgar pointed toward the ceiling and Sarah looked up. The only thing she could guess he was pointing at was one of the holes the smoke was going through. They were too small for Edgar or Jeb to fit through. But not for her. She realized immediately what Edgar had in mind. "Do you have any idea where they go?"

Edgar shrugged. "What else do you do with smoke but send it outside?"

"Okay. Say I can get out. What then?"

Jeb stepped forward. "To the Green Desert. Get the blemmyes. Bring them back here. Get us out. Then we'll all go back to the breach you came through."

Sarah shook her head. "But I don't know how to get to the Green Desert."

In answer, Edgar whipped open his jacket and revealed rows of pockets inside, each containing a folded piece of paper. He ran his fingers along the edges of several, then plucked one free and shook it open. It was a map, drawn in black ink on yellowing paper. It looked terribly old and fragile to Sarah, like a pirate's treasure map.

"But I thought you ate it," she said.

Edgar smiled. "I did. The original. I started work on this copy as soon as Balthazat locked me in here. I didn't want to forget everything I had worked so hard to find."

Sarah smiled, and the three of them moved closer to the wall, holding the map in the light from one of the blue fire torches.

"Tell me what you can remember about where you came through," Edgar said. "What was the landscape like?"

Sarah lifted her fingers to her mouth and started

chewing on her nails, something she always did when she was thinking her hardest.

"It's in the Forest of Shadows," Jeb said. "Just near the River of Moonlight."

"Moonlight?" Sarah said in disbelief. "That silver water is moonlight?"

Jeb nodded. "It flows out to the Moonlit Sea."

"No wonder it was so cold and tasted so . . . sharp," she said.

Edgar and Jeb exchanged glances and then looked back at her grimly.

"You tasted it?" Jeb said.

Sarah nodded slowly. "What if I did?"

Jeb swallowed hard. "That's how Balthazat makes the sentinels."

Sarah suddenly felt cold and wet. She shook her head, trying to deny what they were saying. "You mean I'll turn into one of those things that carries the heads around?"

Jeb nodded.

"How long before that happens?"

"I've only seen it once. He captured a blemmye and made him drink a whole bucket of moonlight. After that, it didn't take long. A day, maybe."

"But I only drank a little bit."

"Then we still have time," Edgar said. "But we better get moving."

Sarah turned away from the two of them, putting her hand to her forehead. "I don't want to turn into one of those things," she said, feeling like she was about to cry. She faced Jeb. "Is there any way to stop it?"

"Only Balthazat would know," Jeb said.

"Oh," Sarah said, turning away from them again. "What are we going to do?"

"Pay attention," Edgar said with such force that Sarah was shocked and a little scared. "That is what you are going to do."

In spite of her fear, she knew he was right. Sometimes you had to take things very seriously. Like when they did fire drills at school. "You're right," she said. "I'm sorry."

Edgar put his hand on her shoulder. "No need to apologize. Just make it up to us by getting us out of here."

Sarah sniffed back her tears and wiped her nose. Then Edgar pointed at the map. "Here's the Forest of Shadows. The River of Moonlight comes from this mountain. This spot here"—Edgar put his finger on an X—"is where you came through. It's the only breach in that area." Sarah nodded. Edgar pointed to another spot on the map. "This is where we are, in the Black Iron Prison. Here is the Moonlit Sea. And here is Crooked Canyon. If you follow that, you can reach the Green Desert and cross it to where the blemmyes are, here."

Edgar handed Sarah the map and she looked at it closely, making sure she had followed everywhere he had pointed.

"Can you do it?" Edgar asked.

"Of course she can," said Jeb. "I know she can."

Sarah looked up at him and smiled. "That settles it, then, huh?" She folded the map and put it in her pocket.

"Almost," Jeb said, lifting his shirt. He took out the glass case containing his face and held it out to her. "Can you take this with you? Keep it safe?"

Sarah frowned and shook her head. "I don't think that's a good idea."

"Of course it is."

"But what if something happens to me?"

"I trust you. Besides, if I keep it here, it's only a matter of time before they search me, find it, and take it away."

Sarah nodded and took the case, suddenly overwhelmed by their faith in her. Yes, it was her fault that all of this had happened. But now she had the chance to undo all the bad things. More than that: to make everything right again. To give Jeb his face back and to free Edgar so that he could return home.

At once, Edgar set to work helping Jeb onto his shoulders. They stood against the wall and then helped Sarah climb up their backs. When she reached Jeb's shoulders, he held on to the base of one of the torch mounts and they carefully leaned away from the wall. Sarah reached one hand into the dark hole. She found an edge and quickly pulled herself up. When she was halfway in, Jeb pushed her feet through, then went back to the wall and climbed down from Edgar's shoulders. The two of them stood on the floor and looked up, waiting to hear what she saw.

"Well?" Edgar said.

The truth was, Sarah could see only darkness. She had half expected to see stars, but then she remembered that the sky in Scotopia had no stars. What if the darkness above her wasn't the sky? Sarah wondered. Then she realized that it didn't matter. This was the only way out. "I can see the sky," Sarah called back to them, hoping they couldn't hear the doubt creeping into her voice. "It's pretty far away, but I can see it."

"Hurry, then, child," Edgar called to her. "Once they find out you are gone, they will send everyone after you."

"Why didn't you tell me that before?" she asked.

"Never mind that. Now hurry."

Sarah waved at them one last time, then faced the darkness and climbed toward it.

CHAPTER 22

A Leap of faith

The smoke vent was long and narrow and seemed to be getting narrower the higher she went. She looked back down but could see only a bare sliver of blue light far below her feet. She inched along, pulling herself with one arm, holding the glass case with Jeb's face tightly in the other. Just when she thought the vent would never end, her fingers found the top edge and she heaved a sigh of relief. Gripping as hard as she could, she pulled herself up. Then she felt a terrible scraping as the glass case with Jeb's face got stuck between the cold stone walls of the smoke vent.

"No," Sarah whispered, worried that their plan would be undone before it even started.

She pushed the case back down again, as hard as she could. It slid free with such force that she nearly dropped it. She tried pulling it up again but realized that it wouldn't fit through with her body at the same time.

Carefully, she lifted her head up and looked over the edge of the smoke vent. She was on a wall overlooking the platform where Mr. Ink had dropped them. Along the wall on the far side, she saw a pair of the squat one-eyed creatures clutching blue torches. Otherwise, the space was empty.

She pulled herself up a little higher and looked over her shoulder. The Moonlit Sea stretched out behind her as far as she could see, just as Edgar had shown her on the map. As she climbed out of the vent, she let the glass case slide down the front of her body to her feet. Sitting on the edge of the vent, she pulled her feet up slowly, little by little, until she could grab the case and pull it free.

As she stood, she was relieved to see that she was on the outer wall. Had she come out near the platform, she would have still been trapped inside the Black Iron Prison. Here on the wall, nothing but air stood between her and the sea below. This was the good news, but it was also the bad news. In order to get away, she had to jump. There was simply no other choice. If she didn't jump, they would never be free.

She tried to remember all the times she had jumped from high places. She remembered the diving board at her friend Molly's house. Although she had been scared to jump at first, she had soon discovered how much fun it was. By the end of that summer, in fact, she had become an expert at jumping on the board hard enough to bounce fairly high. The next summer, she had moved up to the high dive at the Orange Park pool. She had been scared at first with that, too. But once she had done it a few times, Molly's old diving board seemed positively boring. When they had gone camping later, her mom and dad had taken her to a swimming hole with a cliff that was twice as high as the high dive. She hadn't wanted to jump off it at first. Then, finally, on the last day of their stay, she had gotten her nerve up and gone in.

The jump before her now was easily more than three times as high as that cliff at the campground. Even though she knew she had no choice, she still felt scared. Was the moonlight deep enough? Would it act just like water and really catch her fall? What if she swallowed more of it when she went under? That would make her turn into one of those sentinels even faster. Sarah shook her head and took a step backward, away from the wall.

She lifted the glass case and looked at Jeb's face. The eye was closed, as if this small part of him was sleeping. She wished he were with her now. She wished she could hold his hand and they could jump together. Then she decided that this was really the next best thing. So she gripped the case tightly in both hands and ran toward the edge as fast as she could.

The fall seemed impossibly long. The walls of the Black Iron Prison whooshed past her, dark and cold. When at last she plunged into the icy moonlight, she squeezed her eyes shut and held her breath, closing her mouth as tightly as possible. Down, down into the blinding depths she went. The moonlight was not as dense as water, so she went much deeper than she expected. When her feet touched the bottom, she pushed hard and shot toward the surface. When she broke through, she caught a deep breath and paddled hard, pulling herself toward the shore. Some of the moonlight got into her mouth and she winced once again with the sharp taste of it, spitting it out frantically.

It was much harder to swim in the moonlight than in water. The more she flapped her arms and legs, the less progress she seemed to make. She got tired very fast; for a short time she was afraid she wasn't going to make it. Then the waves pushed at her back and her feet found the ground and she walked the rest of the way to the shore.

The moonlight streamed off her body and onto the black sand around her. How strange it was to feel she should be wet and yet still be perfectly dry. She looked behind her at the towering face of the Black Iron Prison and couldn't believe she had jumped from such a height. She thought of Jeb and Edgar still inside the Blue Suite and knew that she must hurry to get them out of there.

She took the map out of her pocket and unfolded it. She retraced the path Edgar had shown her, from the Black Iron Prison to the Moonlit Sea and then along the shoreline to Crooked Canyon and the Green Desert beyond.

She folded the map again and neatly tucked it back into her pocket, then made sure she had a good grip on the glass case with Jeb's face. With one last look over her shoulder, she started up the beach.

CHAPTER 23

A Change of Plans

Eventually the beach gave way to rockier ground and an uphill slope. It would have been easier to leave the beach and head to higher ground, but as far as Sarah could tell from the map, the mouth of Crooked Canyon opened at the sea's edge. So she picked her way over a series of boulders and stuck to the ever-narrowing strip of sand closest to the lapping moonlight.

The ground to her left got higher and higher, rising into the sky at such a steep angle, it began to look like it would fall on her. She saw holes in the rock face that looked like caves and she shivered at the thought of what might live in them. She picked up her pace and finally found what she hoped was the entrance to Crooked Canyon. Just to be sure, she walked across the mouth to the other side, where she discovered it was completely blocked by a pile of fallen boulders. If she wanted to go any farther, she would have

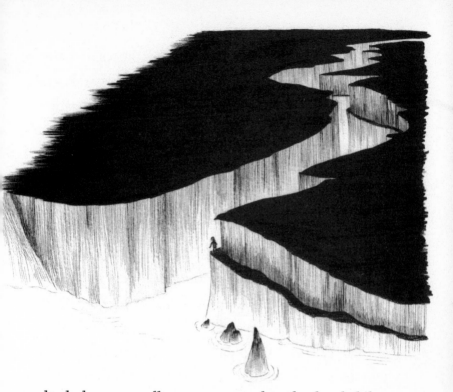

to climb the steep wall or swim around it. She decided that even if this wasn't Crooked Canyon, it *was* the way she was going. She took a deep breath and started along the path.

The walls of the canyon were steep and high. The narrow band of starless sky looked like a dark blue river. Inside the canyon, the sound of the Moonlit Sea crashing onto the shore behind her got even louder. As the path cut to the left and then back to the right again, Sarah began to feel certain that this must be Crooked Canyon. It was certainly crooked enough. With every turn, the Moonlit Sea slipped farther from view and the canyon grew darker.

After getting caught by Mr. Ink, she felt especially scared of the shadows. He could be in any of the pools of darkness; in fact, he could actually be any of the pools of darkness. She shivered at the thought and picked up her pace, trying to concentrate instead on following the path.

"Psst!" something hissed behind her, and Sarah jumped, shrieking. She whirled around quickly and peered into the darkness, her eyes darting back and forth. She stepped backward and caught her foot on a rock, tripped, and sat down hard. The darkness between two rocks shifted and a pair of glowing yellow eyes blinked at her.

"Who's there?" she asked.

The creature, just bigger than her little brother, Billy, waddled into the middle of the path, stood up straight, and stretched its wings open. It was a giant bat, but with a little boy's face. He twitched his ears at her and stepped closer. "I don't know," he said sadly. "I was hoping you could tell me."

All at once, Sarah felt relieved. He wasn't scary, just scared. Maybe even more scared of her than she was of him. "You mean you don't even know your own name?" she said as she got back to her feet.

He looked at her, stretching his wings once more before folding them back at his side, then shook his head. "No," he said.

"My name's Sarah," she said, and held out her hand.

He shook it with the tiny hook at the top of his wing. "Nice to meet you," he said.

"Did you *ever* know your name?"

The bat-boy shrugged. "I don't remember."

"Can you remember anything?"

"Just that I've always been in this place."

"You mean here, in Crooked Canyon?"

"Is that what it's called?"

Sarah nodded and suddenly felt very sad for the little bat-boy. She suspected that he was another of Balthazat's

victims. Like Jeb, only instead of stealing a part of his face, Balthazat had turned him into a giant bat with no memory. She wished there was some way she could help him, too. Then she had an idea. "Can you fly?" she asked.

The bat-boy nodded.

"Have you ever been to the Green Desert?"

He shrugged. "I don't know."

"But if I told you how to get to the Green Desert, you could fly me there, right?"

"I could try."

"If you would help me do that, then maybe I could help you find out your name."

"You could?"

Sarah nodded. "I could try. What do you say?"

"Hop on," the bat-boy said.

"Before I do that, we need to decide what I should call you. Until we find out your real name, I mean. I wouldn't feel right saying 'Hey, you' all the time."

"What would you like to call me?"

Sarah held her chin in one hand and stared at him for a long time. "Well," she said, "you're like a bat and a boy. But 'Bat-Boy' doesn't sound very nice. Suppose I just call you 'B.B.' for short."

"B.B.?"

"What do you think?"

He considered it for a moment, then nodded. "B.B. it is."

Sarah smiled and climbed onto B.B.'s back. The spots not covered with heavy black fur were leathery but warm. "Okay," she said, locking her arms around his thick neck.

"Okay," he said, and spread his wings wide, flapping until they rose into the air. They veered to the left for so long that Sarah thought they were going to crash into the wall. Then B.B. changed course and they veered to the right, coming so close to the top of Crooked Canyon that Sarah's feet knocked some rocks loose. Once they were in the open, B.B. really flapped his wings and they rose even higher into the dark blue sky.

Sarah gasped at the view. The Moonlit Sea lay behind them, stretching out for what seemed like forever. Far back on her left, she could just make out the dark square of the Black Iron Prison.

"Which way?" B.B. yelled above the keening wind.

Sarah faced forward and pointed along the length of Crooked Canyon. "Follow the canyon," she shouted.

"No need to shout," B.B. yelled back at her. "My ears are very sensitive."

She had forgotten learning in school how sensitive bats' ears were. "Sorry," she said, more quietly this time. B.B. nodded and flapped them still higher. Now Sarah could even see the Forest of Shadows, far beyond the Black Iron Prison. All at once, she realized that B.B. could just take her straight there, back to the place where she had come through. She needn't worry about how far above the ground the hole was—B.B. could fly her right in. And if the sentinels or Lefty tried to get her, B.B. could fly her out of their reach. The only one she had to worry about was Mr. Ink, since he could fly, too. But he wouldn't be looking for her there. As far as she knew, he was still at the Black Iron Prison, waiting to see what the guards were going to do with her and Jeb.

She began to wonder if they had discovered she was missing yet. Edgar had said they would send everyone to search for her. She suddenly became sure they would look for her in the Green Desert, since they knew that was where she and Jeb had been headed before Mr. Ink caught them. So maybe she should go back to the Forest of Shadows. She worried about Jeb and Edgar, but she knew the most important thing was stopping Balthazat. Especially since he was the only one who could tell her how to stop from changing into a sentinel. Besides, she wasn't even sure she would be able to convince the blemmyes to start a new rebellion. "Oh, dear," she whispered.

"What is it?" B.B. said.

"I think we better change direction."

"Which way?"

"That way," Sarah said, and pointed left. "To the Forest of Shadows."

B.B. nodded and lifted his right wing. They careened into a sharp turn and Sarah tightened her grip.

As they flew past the Black Iron Prison, Sarah saw a door open and a thin line of squat guards march out. They were so far below that the blue torches they clutched looked like tiny matches. She knew they were searching for her. And from the looks of it, they were headed toward Crooked Canyon and the Green Desert. She heaved a sigh of relief, sure now that she had made the right decision.

On they flew, across the River of Moonlight and deep into the Forest of Shadows. Sarah asked B.B. to take them lower. When she spotted the clearing and Balthazat's cabin, she pointed B.B. toward the face of the black mountains.

As they got closer, Sarah frantically searched the ground for Lefty or the sentinel, but didn't spot any sign of either of them. She knew she should have been relieved, but she actually grew more worried. Not knowing where they were seemed much worse than finding them waiting for her.

"Take us down, please," she said, and B.B. folded his wings back. They plunged toward the ground, and at the last possible moment, B.B. unfolded his wings and brought them to what seemed a complete stop in midair, before setting them down softly. The rapid descent had so frightened Sarah that she hadn't had time to direct B.B. to a close landing position, so when she looked up, she saw that they were still some distance from the mountainside. "This way," she said urgently.

She took off, her feet kicking up black sand as B.B.

waddled behind for a moment, then flapped his wings and flew after her. They reached the mountainside at about the same time. B.B. landed next to her and glanced around.

"What are we doing here?" he asked.

Sarah pointed at the hole in the rock. "Do you see that hole?" she asked. B.B. followed her finger with his eyes and nodded. "I need you to get me up there."

"Sure thing," he said, and motioned for her to climb onto his back. Instead of flying, he used his sharp claws and the hooks at the tops of his wings to crawl up the rocks to the ledge just under the hole. Sarah climbed off and peered into the darkness. Now that she was here, she wasn't sure what to do next. After all, she had completely ditched the original plan.

"What's in there?" B.B. asked.

"My house," Sarah said.

"You live in a cave, too?" B.B. said with a smile. "Can I come with you?"

Sarah explained to him as quickly as she could that this wasn't a normal cave, that it was more like a hallway to a world very different from Scotopia, and that she had to go there and do some very important work. "And I have to go alone," she said.

"But when will you help me find my name?" B.B. asked. "You said you would."

Sarah nodded. "And I will, I promise. Until then, I need you to keep helping me."

"How?"

"I need you to wait here—right here—until I come back. Can you do that?"

"Sure," B.B. said.

Sarah smiled. "Good. I'll be back as fast as I can," she said, then gave B.B. a hug and climbed into the dark tunnel.

CHAPTER 24

Disaster at Home

As Sarah crept back into the secret room behind the
bookcase, her mind raced with a hundred trains of
thought. She wondered if Edgar's theory was true. Had time
stood still while she had been gone? Or had it continued
normally because she had brought Balthazat through?
Had Balthazat figured out where the journal was? Had he
tricked Billy into helping him?

She pushed through the darkness until she felt the
back of the bookcase. Then she pressed against it gently
until it slid out from the wall. When there was enough
space, she peeked through to make sure the coast was
clear. She was about to go into her room when she realized
she was still holding the glass case with Jeb's face in it. She
knew she couldn't take it with her. How could she explain
that to anyone? Carefully, she set the case down against
the wall, then slipped into her bedroom and pushed the

bookcase back into
position.

She let out a deep
breath and looked
around. At first she
thought everything
was exactly as she had
left it, but then she
saw the clock and she
knew Edgar was right.
It was 2:37 p.m. Time *had*
continued normally and
she had been gone for more
than four and a half hours. Feeling
sick with the thought of what might have happened, she
rushed across the room, flung the door open, and ran
downstairs.

She found her mother in the kitchen, standing at the
sink washing potatoes, a red dish towel slung over one
shoulder. "What do you think you're doing, young lady?
Your father told you to stay in your room until dinner." Her
mother looked at the clock over the stove. "And that's not
for more than two hours."

Sarah stopped short and stared at her mom, absolutely
speechless. She didn't know what to say. A part of her

wanted to tell her everything, top to bottom, start to finish. But even as her mouth opened and the first words started to form on her lips, she knew she couldn't. If Sarah told her about secret doors and talking cats, Mom certainly wouldn't believe her. In fact, she would probably send her back to her room for the rest of the day before she called a doctor to come over and find out what was wrong with her. Then Sarah considered that maybe she should instead tell her mom there was a secret room behind the bookcase and get her to go inside that way, but she doubted that would work, either. Mom didn't like small spaces and she was very afraid of spiders. Sarah was sure Mom would refuse to go behind the bookcase for those two reasons and then Sarah would be stuck again. She might be able to convince her dad to go in there, but he would probably tell her he couldn't do it right away and would promise instead to do it tomorrow, which would certainly be too late.

Sarah now realized that she had been staring at her mom for a long time without saying anything, so she finally decided to stick with the simplest explanation, even though it was a lie. "I thought I heard you call me," she said.

Mom lifted her eyebrows. "You did, did you?"

Sarah nodded.

"Well, I didn't," Mom said. "But since you've stayed in

your room this long without complaining and without asking for a break, your punishment can be over."

Sarah was surprised and relieved. "Thanks, Mom," she said, then added as quickly as she could: "Have you seen Balthazat?"

"I think he was outside with Billy."

Sarah felt her stomach drop. "When was that?" she said.

"After lunch, maybe?"

Sarah started toward the back door. "Is Billy still out there?"

"I don't know," Mom said. "He's been coming and going all afternoon. Taking stuff from the room upstairs down to the basement."

Sarah nodded, then stepped onto the back porch and looked around for any sign of Billy or Balthazat. She knew that she had to be careful. As far as Balthazat knew, Sarah still thought he was just the King of the Cats, and she had no intention of letting him find out otherwise. She was fairly certain that if he knew that she knew the truth, he would hurt her somehow, the way he had taken off half of Jeb's face. He might even do something to her whole family.

"Balthazat," she called. "Here, kitty, kitty." She kissed the air as loudly as she could, but heard no reply—not even a meow. She descended the steps to the yard and headed for the bushes along the fence, calling his name and kissing the air. But still she got no reply.

Maybe he was in the basement. After all, Mom had said that Billy had been taking stuff down there. Sarah returned to the house. She went through the back door and down the steps into the basement.

It was dark and silent. "Balthazat?" she called. Still no answer. A new fear took hold of her now. Had Balthazat already accomplished his plan? Had he gotten the door to Penumbra open, stolen the sleeping souls, and taken them back to Scotopia? She didn't see how that was possible, but she couldn't figure out how else to explain Balthazat's absence.

When she turned around, Billy was standing at the top of the stairs, a box in his hands. "Punishment's all over, huh?" he asked.

Sarah nodded. "Have you seen Balthazat?"

"Yeah," Billy said, coming down the stairs. He set his box down on a stack of other boxes. "He scratched me and then ran into the bushes by the fence. I don't know where he went after that and I don't care." Billy went back up the steps and Sarah followed him quickly.

"Can you show me exactly where that happened?"

"No," Billy said. "I hope you never find that cat again. I don't want him to ever come back here."

"Billy!" Mom said from the kitchen. "Don't talk like that."

Billy hung his head. "All right," he said. "Come on." Billy took Sarah outside and around the side of the house, near the basement window. He pointed at the thick bushes along the low fence. "He ran right through there."

"Why did he scratch you?"

"I don't know. We were playing with the piece of string Mom tied to my key."

"Do you still have it?"

"The key or the string?"

"The key."

Billy nodded again and pulled it out of his pocket and showed it to her. Sarah started to reach for it, but Billy closed his hand fast. "It's mine. Mom gave it to me. Do you want to get in trouble again?"

Sarah pulled her hand away. Billy started toward the back door but Sarah said, "Wait. I want to ask you something else."

"What?"

"Did Balthazat talk to you?"

Billy stared at Sarah for a long moment. "What do you mean?"

Sarah shook her head. "Never mind," she said, and forced herself to laugh. "I was just kidding."

"You're weird," Billy said, and went into the house.

Sarah looked into the bushes and whispered Balthazat's name, but the only reply was the crunching of the branches as she pushed them aside with her hands. A moment later, she spotted what must have been the string from Billy's key on the ground and she picked it up. So Balthazat had tried to get the key. When he couldn't, he'd gotten mad, scratched Billy, and taken off. But where was he now? Why wouldn't he come when he heard Sarah calling?

"Sarah," Mom shouted from inside the house. "Come inside now and get back to packing."

"Be right there," Sarah answered. She climbed the steps and opened the door. Before she went inside, she took one last look at the yard, but it was still empty.

Sarah hardly said a word for the rest of the day, including dinner. Instead, she concentrated on trying to figure out where Balthazat could have gone or what he was up to. One possibility was that he had run too far away and someone else had picked him up, thinking he was just a stray cat. If that was the case, hopefully they would do what she and her father had done. When they came to her door with the cat in a box, she could say he was hers and then take him back to Scotopia and figure out how to close off the secret passage forever. It also occurred to her that maybe he had just given up on Billy and had instead gone in search of someone else who could help him. Someone he could convince to break into their house while they were all asleep and steal the key from Billy. This made her so afraid that she started shaking. She shook so hard, a bite of food fell off her fork.

"Are you okay?" Mom asked.

"I'm fine," Sarah said. "I'm just worried about Balthazat."

Dad shook his head. "Maybe it's best if he doesn't come back, honey."

Sarah nodded. Her dad was right, in a way. She wished Balthazat would get run over by a car or something. That would solve all her problems, wouldn't it? She lifted another bite to her mouth, but then decided she wasn't hungry anymore. "Can I be done?" she said.

"You didn't eat very much," Mom said.

"I'm not hungry."

Mom looked at Dad. Dad shrugged. "Fine with me," he said, and Sarah took her plate to the kitchen sink. Then she went outside and sat on the back porch, staring at the yard, kissing the air and calling to Balthazat every few minutes. She simply didn't know what else to do. She couldn't go back to Scotopia now because she still had to take a shower and get ready for bed. She would have to wait until her parents had kissed her good night before she could go behind the bookcase again.

When it got dark, Mom called her inside.

After her shower, she put her pajamas on and climbed into bed with a book. Then Mom and Dad came in. After kisses, they went out of her room and closed the door all the way. She listened to them tuck Billy in and then go downstairs. A few minutes later, as soon as she heard the TV go on, she threw the covers back and got dressed.

CHAPTER 25

The Truth At Last

She had just started to pull the bookcase out of the wall when she heard a click in the hallway. She froze. Then she shoved the bookcase back into the wall, dove into bed, and pulled the covers up as fast as she could. She was sure Mom or Dad had come back upstairs to check on her for some reason. She held her breath as she waited for her door to open. When she heard a second click, she realized that it wasn't her door, it was Billy's.

She threw the covers back again and crept across the room as quickly and carefully as she could. She knelt in front of her door, peering through the keyhole. The hallway was dark except for the glow of the night-light from the bathroom. Still, that was enough light to see that Billy's bedroom door was opening very slowly. And now Billy was peering out. He opened the door wider. He, too, had gotten dressed. He had the key in one hand and the big red book in the other. All at once Sarah knew that her brother had lied to her. Not only did Balthazat know about the journal, but he had talked to Billy, too. Now her brother was sneaking down to meet the cat in the basement and open the door to Penumbra for him. That was why Balthazat hadn't answered. He didn't need her anymore. He was probably hiding down there—and had been all afternoon—waiting for this moment.

Sarah was very tempted to throw the door open and yell for Mom and Dad. She and Billy would both get in big trouble for being dressed and out of bed, but at least she would stop Balthazat from going through with his plan. She was just about to open her mouth when she realized that she could only catch Balthazat if she let Billy meet him. So she held her breath and watched Billy sneak to the corner of the hallway and disappear from view.

She waited a long moment, then opened her door wide and poked her head out. She could just see his shadow descending the stairs. She couldn't believe he was risking this. Mom and Dad were almost sure to catch him. She waited until she couldn't see his shadow on the wall anymore, then crept out of her room and closed the door.

She tiptoed up the hallway and looked over the railing. She saw Billy at the bottom of the stairs, peeking around the corner, into the living room, no doubt making sure

Mom and Dad couldn't see him. After a moment, he darted into the kitchen, out of Sarah's sight.

Sarah went to the landing and was halfway downstairs when she heard Dad get up and tell Mom he would be right back. She backed up quickly, crouching in the shadows at the top of the stairs. She watched Dad walk into the kitchen. Every muscle tightened as she waited to hear Dad shout at Billy, but all she heard was the ice maker crunching ice into a glass and the pop of a soda can being opened. A moment later, Dad walked back into the living room.

Sarah let out her breath and went down the stairs on her tiptoes. At the bottom, she peered into the living room and saw Mom and Dad facing the TV, watching an old black-and-white movie. She went into the kitchen carefully, half afraid that she would find Billy coming out from a hiding place somewhere. But the kitchen was empty. Assuming that he had already gone into the basement, Sarah went to the door and opened it carefully. She saw light—from a flashlight—sweep across the far wall. She stepped onto the landing and closed the door.

Even more carefully than before, Sarah went down the stairs. She lowered her head, trying to see where Billy was. The light flashed again, this time sweeping across the stacks of furniture and crates near the boiler. She moved down the stairs more quickly.

Once she reached the bottom, she crouched and crept forward to a row of boxes. Peeking over the top, she saw Billy, alone, standing at the door behind the boiler. One hand held the flashlight trained on the heavy padlock while the other hand lifted the key and put it in the lock. When she still saw no sign of Balthazat, she decided that Billy must have already let him into Penumbra but had been forced to close and lock the door when Mom had come downstairs or something.

Sarah crept forward another inch as Billy turned the key in the lock and popped it open. He pulled the padlock off and set it on the ground along with the journal. Then he pulled the heavy door open to reveal an alcove filled with dim light. Another door stood on the opposite side, a good twenty feet away. This door looked older than the first, and it was not locked.

Then Billy said, "Hello, Billy," and Sarah nearly fell over. Her breath caught in her throat and she slowly lifted herself high enough to see the alcove floor. There, bound hand and foot with yellow nylon rope, was her little brother. He was staring at the other Billy with wide eyes. But the worst part of all was that the Billy who was tied up on the floor had no mouth.

Sarah very nearly screamed then. To stop herself, she had to bite her tongue and squeeze her eyes shut. Now she

knew the truth: the Billy who had met her on the stairs that afternoon had not been her brother at all. Balthazat had simply changed disguises. He had lured Billy into the basement and gotten the door open. Then he had changed into Billy, tied the real Billy up, and waited until he could come back to finish the job.

Sarah was frantic. If Balthazat could change into Billy like that, who knew what else he could do? If she screamed for help, might he not simply turn into a giant dragon and destroy them all with a single breath of fire? One thing she knew for certain: she couldn't leave Billy behind, no matter how annoying he was.

She crept forward slowly, taking cover behind the boxes and furniture. She got as close to the first door as she dared, then waited as Balthazat went to the inner door and opened it. Beyond it was a giant space, as dimly illuminated by dark gray light as the alcove, filled with rows and rows of what looked like thousands of beds. People covered with white sheets lay on the beds, which seemed to stretch on as far as she could see, up a gentle slope of gray grass.

Balthazat—still in his disguise as Billy—stood in the open doorway, his arms outstretched.

"At last," he said. "Penumbra!"

Sarah took advantage of his distraction to dart forward and grab the real Billy. When he saw her, his eyes went wide.

She tried to help him to his feet, but halfway up, he stumbled and fell, pushing them both back. Balthazat heard the noise and whirled around. His face was no longer Billy's. Instead, his hair had turned to smoke and his eyes to fire. Sarah closed the door, snatched the lock from the ground, and put it through the latch. Balthazat pushed on the door from the inside, but Sarah snapped the lock shut. She held her breath, afraid Balthazat would start pounding on the door from the inside and bring Mom and Dad down, but instead he only whispered, "I'll find another way out, little girl. Don't you know that? My plan will succeed, and I have you to thank for it." At the sound of his voice, goose bumps crowded the back of Sarah's neck.

But she had no time to be scared.

She turned to Billy and quickly untied the ropes. She did her best to explain to him that she knew what had happened and that she would tell him more soon. "But for now," she whispered, "we have to get back upstairs without Mom and Dad knowing. Can you do that?"

He nodded.

"Good," she said. Then she took the key from the lock, picked up the journal, and grabbed Billy by the hand. "Come on."

CHAPTER 26

Grandma Winnie Explains It All

Sarah stopped short when she saw someone coming down the stairs. She couldn't tell whether it was Mom or Dad. Not that it mattered. Either one spelled bad news, although Mom would probably not be as likely to yell. They must have heard her and Billy down here. Now everything would come out. What would they say when they saw Billy's face?

Sarah sighed. Maybe this was for the best. She was tired of trying to make everything right all on her own. Briefly, she considered hiding, then decided that would only make things worse.

Standing up as straight as she could, she stepped out and came face to face not with her mom or dad, but with Grandma Winnie.

Sarah screamed.

"Oh, no, child," Grandma said to her. "I wish you hadn't done that."

Sarah's mouth opened and closed, but no words came out. She looked at Billy. But Billy just stared at her as if he couldn't figure out what was happening.

Sarah heard voices overhead, followed by footsteps pounding from the living room to the kitchen. Mom and Dad were coming for sure.

"Quick," Grandma Winnie said, "you and your brother stand behind me and get under my shawl."

Sarah grabbed Billy and pulled him close. Then Grandma turned around. She whipped her shawl off her shoulders and draped it over them like a magician. All at once, Sarah realized she could see through Grandma Winnie and she wanted to scream again, but then the light went on and Mom and Dad came down the stairs.

"I swear I heard someone scream," Mom said.

"Me too," Dad said. "It sounded like Sarah."

Her parents were staring straight at her and Billy and Grandma Winnie, but it was obvious they couldn't see them. Then, as they stepped to the floor, Grandma Winnie moved forward, floating, carrying Sarah and Billy with her. They glided right past Mom and Dad, and as they went upstairs, Sarah heard Dad say, "Maybe we should check on the children."

"That's a good idea," Mom said.

Sarah looked over her shoulder and saw them headed

back to the stairs, but then Grandma floated around the corner and up to their rooms.

"Quickly now," Grandma said. "Both of you get in your beds and pretend you're asleep."

Sarah and Billy did as she told them. And not a

moment too soon, for Sarah had barely pulled the covers to her chin when her door opened and Mom and Dad leaned through.

"She in there?" Dad asked.

"Sound asleep," Mom said, and closed the door.

Sarah jumped out of bed and peered through the keyhole, watching her parents repeat the routine at Billy's door. A few moments later, they headed downstairs.

Sarah leaned back and caught her breath, her mind racing with what had just happened. When her door opened and Billy came in, she was actually glad to see him, and evidently he felt the same way. They hugged each other tightly.

"Is Grandma Winnie with you?" Sarah asked.

Billy looked at her and shook his head.

"Did you see Grandma Winnie?"

Again, Billy shook his head.

"Oh," Sarah said, confused. Then it dawned on her: she had been holding the journal and the key. Jeb had told her that they only worked together, and only when they were together could the record keeper show the sleeping dead the way to Penumbra.

Sarah jumped to her feet and ran to her bed. She threw the covers back and grabbed the journal and the key. When she turned around, she saw Grandma Winnie standing in the corner. Sarah heaved a sigh of relief. "There you are," she whispered.

"You had me worried," Grandma said. "I thought I was going to have to start throwing letters around and banging books on the floor again."

"That was you?" Sarah asked.

Grandma nodded. "I was trying to get your attention. I started as soon as you got here."

Sarah smiled. "I knew it," she said. "Was that you last night at the door, too?"

Grandma shook her head slowly. "Those are all the sleeping dead. They're here because it's their time to enter Penumbra, but I can't let them in, because, well, look at me."

"You mean there are dead people outside?"

Grandma nodded and went to the window. Sarah followed her and looked down. In the yard below, their forms outlined by the silver moonlight, were about two dozen people shuffling aimlessly around the yard. "They'll knock again at three o'clock. Just like they've been doing every night."

Billy appeared next to Sarah and looked out the window. Seeing nothing but the empty yard, he shrugged. "Oh," Sarah said. "You can't see them, can you?"

Billy shook his head.

Sarah said, "Here," and shoved the journal and key

toward him. He touched the key with one hand and the journal with the other. When he looked out the window again his eyes widened. Sarah was quite sure that if he'd had a mouth, he would have been smiling and saying "Cool!" in that annoying and reverential tone.

She shook her head and turned to Grandma again. "So what do we do?"

"We've got to get them into Penumbra."

Sarah nodded, then realized that that simply wasn't possible—not with Balthazat in there. She looked at the floor.

"What is it, child?" Grandma asked.

"I'm afraid I've made some big mistakes," Sarah said. She took a deep breath and explained how she had found Scotopia and how she had thought Balthazat was her friend. Then she told them about Jeb and how he had made her see the truth: Balthazat only wanted to get into Penumbra so he could steal the sleeping souls who really belonged in Ormaz. She told Billy not to worry about his missing mouth because Balthazat had taken half of Jeb's face, but she was sure they would figure out a way to put both of them back the way they were.

Just then, the bookcase slowly came out of the wall, scraping across the floor. Sarah and Billy and Grandma all looked at each other, then looked back at the bookcase. It edged forward again. For a moment, Sarah thought

she should throw herself against it and stop whoever—
or whatever—it was from getting through. But it was too
late. The bookcase slid out farther and she saw the hooked
tip of B.B.'s wing poke through just before she heard him
whisper, "Sarah? Are you in there?"

Sarah let a breath out. "It's okay," she whispered. "It's
B.B. I'm trying to help him, too."

She let Billy hold the key and the journal and pulled the
bookcase out far enough to let B.B. in. He waddled into her
room and glanced around. "Boy, am I glad to see you," he
said. "I know you told me to wait down there for you, but I
couldn't. Not when I saw those other things show up."

"What other things?" Sarah asked.

"A giant hand and a guy carrying a head."

"Lefty and one of the sentinels. Did they see you?"

B.B. shook his head. "I heard them coming and I
backed into the tunnel. Once I actually saw them, I knew
they were bad."

"What did they do?"

B.B. shook his head again. "I didn't stay around long
enough to see. I was so worried, all I could think about was
finding you. So I climbed up and here I am."

Sarah nodded. "You did the right thing. But if they're
down there guarding the entrance, how are we going to get
back to Scotopia?"

B.B. looked at her sadly. "Does this mean you won't be able to help me find out my real name?"

"No," Sarah said. "I will. It just might take longer than I thought." She sat down on the edge of the bed and hit her head with her palms. "Think, think, think," she said. "I know that Jeb got through from a different house. And Edgar found a lot of ways in." She pulled the map from her pocket and unfolded it. "But his map just shows where the doors are inside Scotopia." Sarah sighed. "If only there were some way we could get back to Scotopia, I could get help from the blemmyes or Edgar."

Billy came over and tapped Sarah on the shoulder frantically.

"Leave me alone, Billy, I'm trying to think." But he only tapped harder. When she finally looked at him, she saw he was shoving the journal and the key at her.

She grabbed them both and Grandma Winnie popped into view.

"You must go to Ormaz," she said.

"Ormaz," Sarah said with a nod, remembering how Jeb had told her it was the place where light comes from. If anyone would know how to fight shadows, it would be someone there. "That's a good idea, Grandma," Sarah said. "But how do I get there?"

"Use the other door."

"What other door?" Sarah asked.

"In the blue room, where your brother is staying. The passage behind his bookcase leads to Ormaz."

"Of course it does," she said, and together they all moved as quickly and quietly as they could into Billy's room.

Billy had already taken all the books off the shelves. So Sarah simply grabbed the middle shelf and pulled as hard as she could.

Nothing happened.

Her shoulders sagged. Then she tried again. She grabbed the middle shelf and pulled hard.

"Maybe I'm not strong enough," she said. "Can you help, B.B.?"

B.B. waddled forward and put the hooks at the tips of his wings on the outer edge of the bookcase. He pressed them between the wood and the wall, then tugged outward. There was a cracking sound, and at last the bookcase came free.

Relieved, Sarah wiped her forehead. "Thanks, B.B.," she said, pulling the bookcase out the rest of the way. She peered into the space expecting to see the same kind of darkness as behind her bookcase. But instead, she saw light shining down at the back. She smiled and looked at the others. Then she took the journal and key from Billy and asked Grandma if she could come with her.

"No, child," Grandma Winnie said. "I can't. I hope I'll be able to someday. But until then, I'm supposed to be in Penumbra."

Sarah nodded, then faced Billy and B.B. "You two better go back to the other side and keep watch. If anyone tries to come through from Scotopia, come over here and find me. I'll be back as soon as I can."

"Are you sure that's a good idea?" B.B. asked.

"It's all we've got," she said, then slipped behind Billy's bookcase and walked toward the light.

CHAPTER 27

To the Court of the Cloud Queen

Ormaz was nothing like she had expected. When Sarah slid out of the tunnel, she found herself floating in the air right in front of a giant cloud. She looked down and saw no ground at her feet, just clouds drifting past. When they parted, she saw the biggest, brightest ocean ever, even brighter than the Moonlit Sea in Scotopia. Not knowing what else to do, she flapped her arms gently and twisted her body around. Clouds moved past her on every side, even high above her. The sky she floated in was a delicate pale blue. Sarah smiled. How she had ever thought dark old Scotopia was any fun at all, she didn't know.

Suddenly, Sarah noticed that the cloud she had come through was slowly moving away from her. She flapped her arms and pushed herself toward it. She grabbed it and found that it felt like cotton. For a moment, she had a grip, but as it moved away from her and she pulled harder, the cloud tore. She let the small piece go and it floated away. She flapped her arms again and pushed herself up, back toward the hole she had come through. Only, now she saw that it was slowly closing up, getting smaller and smaller as the cloud continued moving away from her. She got near the hole and tried to pull it back open, panicking. If that hole closed, would she ever be able to get back home? She tried to climb in, but it was too late. The hole closed completely, and the pieces of cloud that tore off in her hands floated away like dandelion seeds after a wish has been made.

She stopped flapping and simply floated, watching helplessly as the cloud joined with another and made a bigger cloud.

"What am I going to do now?" Sarah said out loud.

"Hold perfectly still," a voice behind her said, and Sarah let out a little yelp of fright. She started to turn around but the voice got louder. "DO NOT MOVE!" it boomed.

Sarah froze. She was beginning to think this hadn't been such a good idea after all, when a giant bag made of white feathers slipped over her head and closed off at her feet. A moment later, the bag turned over and so did she. She barely managed to right herself before it took off.

"Excuse me," she called. "But who are you and where are you taking me?"

"My name is Dogsbody and I am taking you where all intruders are taken: to the court of the Cloud Queen."

"But Mr. Dogsbody, sir, I'm not an intruder. I came here in search of help."

"Tell it to the Cloud Queen," Dogsbody said, and picked up speed.

"Can you please just tell me if I'm in Ormaz?"

"Of course you are," Dogsbody shouted, and Sarah felt some small measure of relief.

On and on they flew, and after a while Sarah began to consider that maybe this was the best thing that could have happened to her. After all, she had come to Ormaz in search of someone who could help, and now she was apparently being taken to just such a person—a queen, no less.

"Mr. Dogsbody, sir?" Sarah called through the feather bag. "Is the Cloud Queen the ruler of Ormaz?"

"You don't know much, do you?"

"I don't know *that*."

"Yes," he said. "She is. So now you do know it. And just in time, too. We're here."

Sarah felt the bag land on something soft and springy. She waited for Dogsbody to open the bag, but he didn't. She could hear him talking with someone, but she couldn't make out what they were saying. A moment later, somebody poked her through the bag.

"You in there. What's your name?"

"Sarah. Sarah Steiner."

She heard more muffled voices outside the bag, but she still couldn't make out what was being said. Not wanting to wait any longer, she dug into the bag until she found the top and ripped through it, tearing the feathers apart, making a hole big enough to climb through.

As she stood up and pushed the bag down, she found herself standing on a cloud surrounded by other clouds. She heard whispers and gasps, but she couldn't see anyone—or anything, for that matter—other than clouds. She blinked and stared and at last she began to see small movements in the clouds. Then she realized they weren't clouds—they were people.

One cloud separated from the others and floated toward her. As it got closer, Sarah saw that it was a woman, with long flowing cloud hair and pale cloud skin and a cloud dress as blindingly white as snow under sunshine.

"My," the cloud woman said, "you are a spirited one, aren't you?"

"Who are you?" Sarah said, as whole rows of cloud people came forward: cloud men with flowing cloud beards and cloud suits as white as the dresses of the cloud women with them.

"I am the Cloud Queen," said the one who had spoken, and now Sarah noticed the woman had a small cloud crown on top of her flowing cloud hair. "And you, Sarah Steiner," the Cloud Queen said, "I suspect you must be the young relative of one of the record keepers, is that not true? Tell us: how did you get here?"

"Through a secret door behind the bookcase in my brother's bedroom."

The Cloud Queen shook her head. "Just like that?" she asked.

Sarah began to feel nervous. The Cloud Queen seemed to be getting mad. "I don't understand what you mean," Sarah said, her voice barely a whisper.

"Speak up," said the Cloud Queen.

"I don't understand," Sarah repeated, louder.

"That much is obvious," the Cloud Queen said. "Because, young lady, if you understood anything at all, you would not be here. I'll have Dogsbody return you. We will make you fall asleep, and when you wake up you will be back in your bed with the feeling that this was all a dream." The Cloud Queen started to turn away.

"Wait—please!" Sarah said. "I came here for help."

The Cloud Queen stopped and turned around. "What do you mean? Help with what?"

"Something terrible has happened," Sarah said. She was so afraid of making the Cloud Queen mad that she was whispering again.

The Cloud Queen frowned. "Did you say that something terrible has happened?"

Sarah nodded. "Well, you see . . . I didn't come here—

to Ormaz, I mean—first." When Sarah said this, a murmur rose among the cloud people.

"Silence," the Cloud Queen hissed, and they all did exactly as she said. "Go on."

"I went behind my bookcase. The one in my room, I mean. That one took me to a different place. One called Scotopia."

A collective gasp burst from the cloud people. But the Cloud Queen said nothing. Instead, she just stared at Sarah, waiting.

Sarah didn't know what to do except continue. "I'm afraid Balthazat tricked me. He pretended to be a cat and I brought him home with me." The Cloud Queen closed her eyes. Sarah kept on. "He got into Penumbra," she said, and the cloud people began to shriek.

"Dogsbody," the Cloud Queen said, "clear the court at once, then wait outside."

CHAPTER 28

A Taste of Sunlight

Dogsbody, who Sarah now saw was a cloud person like all the others, did as the Cloud Queen ordered. As he led all the cloud people through a door in the clouds, the Cloud Queen took Sarah to a bench made of clouds and they sat down together.

"Now, child," said the Cloud Queen, "tell me the whole story from the beginning to the end."

Sarah did so, as quickly as she could; she was growing anxious. Not just because Balthazat might be going through with his plan, and not just because she was slowly turning into a sentinel, but because she couldn't stop thinking about all the people who were depending on her: B.B. and Edgar and Jeb and Billy and Grandma Winnie and all the dead people wandering around outside.

"Well," the Cloud Queen said when Sarah was finished.

"That is quite a story, the likes of which I can honestly say I have never heard."

"I'm sorry," Sarah said.

"As am I. From what you have told me, a terrible mistake has been made."

"What do you mean?"

"Well, first of all, no record keeper is supposed to go to Penumbra without leaving the job to someone else. It sounds like your grandmother wasn't prepared for that." The Cloud Queen shook her head. "I suppose it's amazing we don't have more problems like this. It's too bad I can't do anything to help you."

Sarah felt like she had been pinched, hard. "What do you mean you can't help me?"

"Just that, I'm afraid. As your friend Jeb told you, we are all forbidden to cross over. You should not have gone to Scotopia, and your grandmother should not have told you to come here. Every time someone crosses over, the balance is upset. Not just in our world here, but in Penumbra and Scotopia, and in your world as well."

"I don't understand."

The Cloud Queen nodded. "Everything was once like this," she said, waving her arm. "Even all those who are now in Scotopia."

Sarah's eyes widened with disbelief. "You mean Balthazat was once a cloud person like you?"

"Yes," the Cloud Queen said. "But he and Leedo and Tantalus and a bunch of others tried to take over. They didn't like the way I ran things. They thought they could do better. So they started a rebellion. Only, they didn't realize what they were doing until it was too late."

"What were they doing?"

"Making darkness. Their rebellion created Scotopia, and their confusion about right and wrong has locked them all away in it. That's why Balthazat can't find a way out on his own."

"Oh," Sarah said, feeling even worse now.

"That's why we're here and they are there. It's also why Balthazat wants to bring some of the sleeping souls who belong to Ormaz with him. He believes they will give him light."

"Won't they?"

"Not in the way he thinks. He believes if he has something there that belongs here, he will make Scotopia a little bit like Ormaz. But he doesn't see that his lying and thievery make that impossible."

Sarah nodded. "So what am I going to do?"

"That you will have to decide for yourself." The Cloud Queen stood and called Dogsbody in.

"But wait," Sarah said. "Aren't you worried about what might happen if Balthazat does what he's trying to do?"

The Cloud Queen shook her head. "You are the one who should be worried. If he succeeds in upsetting the balance by getting some souls from Penumbra, then the doors will open and stay open, and your world will eventually become one with Scotopia."

Sarah felt a wave of nausea wash through her like cold water. "What will happen to you?"

"Nothing," said the Cloud Queen. "We've done nothing wrong."

Sarah felt frantic. There had to be something she could do.

"What about the moonlight I drank?" she asked. "Do you know how I can stop from turning into one of those sentinels?"

The Cloud Queen smiled. "That," she said, "I *can* help you with. Come here."

Sarah rushed forward and the Cloud Queen opened a door in the floor. Beneath it was a shimmering pool, shining so brightly that Sarah held her hand up to her eyes.

"Take a sip of this."

"What is it?" Sarah asked.

"Sunlight, of course. The only cure for moonlight."

Sarah stepped forward and got to her knees. She dipped her hand in the pool and was surprised to find that it was warm. In spite of everything, she smiled as she scooped up some of the sunlight and brought it to her mouth. The warmth was comforting as it swished in her mouth and went down her throat. She felt it spreading through her stomach in waves, pushing away the nausea and the fear. In fact, she suddenly felt better than she had since she couldn't remember when. Overcome with excitement, she dipped her hand toward the pool again, but the Cloud Queen stopped her.

"No, dear," the Cloud Queen said. "That's all you need."

"Please," said Sarah. "Just one more sip."

In answer, the Cloud Queen closed the door. Sarah dropped her hand, disappointed but still feeling energized and hopeful.

"Am I really cured?" she asked.

"Essentially. It will take a bit for the sunlight to push all the moonlight out. But as long as you don't drink any more moonlight, then you should be fine."

Sarah shook her head. "Believe me, I'm not drinking any more moonlight."

"Good," said the Cloud Queen. "Are you ready to go back now?"

Sarah nodded, then said quickly, "Can I ask one more favor?"

"What is it now?"

"Can you not put me to sleep and make me think this was all a dream? I need to remember everything you said."

The Cloud Queen considered her request for a long moment, then nodded once.

"Thank you," Sarah said.

"Away, then," the Cloud Queen said, lifting her arm as if in blessing. "May the water and light follow you."

Sarah waved as the Cloud Queen lowered her arm, turned, and strolled across the courtyard.

Sarah waited until she was gone, then looked at Dogsbody. "Do you have to put me in the bag again?"

"I suppose not," he said.

"Good," Sarah said. Dogsbody bent over and picked her up. A moment later, they shot into the sky.

As they flew away from the courtyard, Sarah looked over her shoulder and saw that they had been in the courtyard of a giant castle built of clouds. Towers and turrets and walls rose up as far as she could see, glittering and white. The farther away they flew, the more of the castle she could see, until she realized she could not see its top or its sides. It seemed to Sarah that the cloud castle was bigger even than all of New York City. And she had seen that from the window of an airplane the summer before.

She felt Dogsbody diving down and she faced forward just as they landed on a cloud. He set her down and pointed at a large hole in front of them. "Right through there," he said. "But hurry now, before it closes up."

Sarah could hardly believe it. "You mean you know all the places to get through?"

"Of course," said Dogsbody.

"But I don't understand."

"We can know because we will never go through them."

Sarah nodded slowly. "And Balthazat can't because he will."

Dogsbody nodded.

"Thank you, Dogsbody," she said. "And tell the Cloud Queen the same thing."

He nodded and she dove into the hole.

CHAPTER 29

Another Way Through

Sarah hadn't realized how bright Ormaz was until she crawled into the darkness at the end of the tunnel. When she pulled herself over the ledge and into the secret room behind Billy's bookcase, she sat still, blinking her eyes, getting used to the dark.

After a moment, she got to her feet and went into Billy's room. It was just as she had left it. In fact, Billy and B.B. were still there.

"What are you guys doing?" she whispered at them. "I told you to go stand guard in my room."

Billy and B.B. looked at each other. "That's where we're going," B.B. said. "What are you doing? I thought you were going to see if you could get help."

Sarah opened her mouth to say that she had already done that, when she remembered what Edgar had told her about time standing still. She smiled excitedly. "Of course!" she said. "That's exactly what happened."

"What happened?"

"Come with me," Sarah said. "I'll explain it to you on our way back to Scotopia."

Billy and B.B. nodded and followed her across the dark hallway to her room.

She held on to the journal and the key as she told Billy and B.B. about Edgar's time theory and how her visit to Ormaz proved it. She also told them about her meeting with the Cloud Queen and how the queen had said it was up to her to stop Balthazat.

"All of us, you mean," B.B. said. "It's up to all of us."

Sarah nodded. "Thank you, B.B.," she said.

"I just wish there were something I could do," Grandma Winnie said.

"But you've already helped," Sarah said. "The trip to Ormaz was the answer to everything. Go downstairs and tell all those poor souls outside that it won't be much longer before they'll be let into Penumbra."

Grandma Winnie's eyes brightened. "I knew you were the one," she said.

"What does that mean?" Sarah asked.

"The new record keeper," Grandma Winnie said. "Your

mother never understood what I was trying to tell her. She had other ideas."

"You mean she was supposed to take over?"

Grandma Winnie nodded. "I had hoped so, anyway."

"But what will we do? Mom and Dad are going to sell the house and then we're going back to California."

"Not if I can help it."

Sarah smiled as Grandma Winnie winked at her and then went through the door and was gone.

Billy held out his hand, palm down, and Sarah knew at once what he wanted. She put her hand on top of his, also palm down. B.B. looked at both of them and then leaned forward so he could put the hook at the tip of his wing on top of both of their hands.

"All in?" Sarah asked.

"Yes," B.B. said. "Now let's get back to work."

Sarah nodded and stood. She took the journal and the key and shoved them under her mattress. Then she told Billy to stick close by her side as the three of them went behind the bookcase.

The hole was too small for all of them to jump through together. They would have to go one at a time. Sarah told B.B. to go first so that he could park himself at the exit and stop her and Billy from falling to the ground, where Lefty and the sentinel could get them. B.B. agreed and jumped into the hole.

"Ooof!" he said from the darkness below.

Sarah leaned over the edge and peered down. "B.B.? Are you okay?"

"Yes," he said, his voice muffled.

"What is it? What's happened?"

"It's blocked."

"What do you mean?"

"I mean the tunnel has been stopped up with something. Rocks, I think."

Sarah put her hand over her mouth. The only explanation she could think of was that Balthazat had already found another way through from Penumbra. He had found another house with three doors and had used it to start transferring the sleeping souls. Knowing that Sarah might try to come through this way, he had ordered the passage blocked to stop her. Sarah called B.B. out of the tunnel and explained her suspicions.

"Come on," she said.

"Where are we going?"

"We have to find another way through."

"What about the basement? Couldn't we go through the door to Penumbra and find where Balthazat went through?"

"No," Sarah said. "Balthazat probably thinks that's what

we'll do when we find this passage blocked. He probably has sentinels waiting for us there. We need to find a completely new way through."

"But how?"

"Back to Ormaz."

Billy and B.B. went out ahead of her and Sarah started to follow, but then stopped short. "Oops," she said. "I almost forgot." She bent down to pick up the glass case with Jeb's face in it, but she couldn't find it.

B.B. poked his head back through. "Aren't you coming?"

"In a minute," Sarah said. "Pull the bookcase out. I need some more light."

B.B. did, but even with the extra light, Sarah still couldn't find Jeb's face.

"What's wrong?" B.B. asked.

"I left something here. A glass box."

"Oh, that?" B.B. said. "I hope it wasn't important."

Sarah felt her stomach drop. "It's very important. Do you know what happened to it?"

B.B. backed up slowly, now looking very worried and upset. "I'm sorry, Sarah," he said. "But when I was climbing through earlier, I knocked it down the tunnel with my wing. I was too scared about the giant hand and the guy with the head in a sling to try to get it back."

Sarah's stomach dropped still further. Now that the

tunnel was blocked, they couldn't even check to see if Lefty or the sentinel had found it.

"What was it, anyway?"

Sarah could see how upset B.B. was. And she also knew that what had happened was an accident. "Let's worry about it later," she said, and went into her room.

With B.B.'s help, she closed the bookcase back up; then all three of them returned to Billy's room and slid through the tunnel, into Ormaz.

Just like before, as soon as they slid through, Dogsbody was there with his feather bag. "You," he said. "What are you doing here again? Who are they?"

"We need your help, Dogsbody," Sarah said. "You need to take us to another way over."

Dogsbody shook his head. "You know I can't do that."

"But you're not the one going through. It'll just be us."

Dogsbody stared at her.

"Please," Sarah said. "There's no time to explain everything that's happened. I think Balthazat has already found another way through, and if we can't get back to Scotopia, we'll never be able to stop him."

"I need to ask the Cloud Queen," he said.

"There's no time for that, either." Dogsbody stared at her and she stared back, her eyes pleading with him. "Please," she went on, "can't you help us just this little bit?

So B.B. can get his name back and my brother can get his mouth back?"

At last Dogsbody nodded. "This way," he said, and picked up Sarah and Billy. "You," he said to B.B., "look like you don't need me to carry you, right?"

"Right," B.B. said, and flapped his wings.

Dogsbody took off into the clouds, flying over some and under others until they reached a flat field of clouds with a small cloud hill in the middle. They landed on the hill and Dogsbody put Sarah and Billy down. He pointed at a hole.

"That's the next closest way through."

Sarah thanked him and then pushed Billy and B.B. through ahead of her. She took one last look at Ormaz, then blew Dogsbody a kiss and climbed in.

The darkness at the end of the tunnel was so complete that she didn't know which way to go. She thrust her hands in front of her, waving them around, trying to find something solid.

"Over here," B.B. whispered, and Sarah followed his voice. "I think this is the way through."

Sarah pushed against the wall and it creaked.

"Let me try," B.B. said, and Sarah stepped aside. He threw his weight into it and the wall opened up. The bookcase, just like in Sarah's and Billy's rooms, slid forward and fell with a thunderous crash. "Oops," B.B. said.

The three of them froze, staring at a room that was exactly the same as Billy's room, only it wasn't Billy's room. And the old man standing in front of them was nothing like Billy.

"Oh, my," the old man said with a foreign accent. "I've been waiting for something like this to happen."

Sarah looked at Billy and B.B., then back at the old man. "I'm sorry," she said.

"It's my fault," said B.B. "I shouldn't have pushed so hard."

The old man stepped toward them. "That bookcase is the least of our problems," he said. "I'm guessing that you are Sarah Steiner?"

Sarah nodded. "How did you know that?"

"A message went out yesterday," he said. "You're from the house in Pennsylvania, aren't you?"

"Isn't that where we are?"

The old man shook his head. "This house is in London."

"England?" Sarah said. For a moment, she didn't believe him. But then she remembered what the Cloud Queen had told her. "Of course," she said, stepping forward and going to the window. "These houses are all over the world. With record keepers like you living in them. That's what you are, right?"

The old man nodded. "They warned us you might come through anywhere. And they said if I see you, I'm supposed to stop you."

"If you stop us," Sarah said, "Balthazat will succeed for sure."

"Who?"

"Balthazat," Sarah said. "The King of Scotopia. If you don't let us go back there, the whole world will go dark."

"That's already happening because of what you've done!" the old man shouted. "I can't let you leave. I can't let you make things worse than they already are."

"You'll have to," Sarah said. "Hold him, B.B."

For a moment, B.B. looked surprised. But then he realized what Sarah was telling him and he moved forward quickly. He spread his wings wide and wrapped the old man in them, clicking his hooks together for the tightest grip possible.

"Let me go!" the old man said, struggling to get free.

"In a minute," Sarah said, and flung the bedroom door open.

She saw immediately that the house was identical to the one they were living in. The other bedroom, just like hers, was across from the one they were in.

"This way," she said. Billy ran ahead of her. B.B. waddled after, the old man still squirming in his wings.

Billy grabbed the edge of the bookcase and pulled it from the wall.

Sarah smiled. "Thanks, Billy," she said. "We better let B.B. go first, just in case."

"What about him?" B.B. asked.

"Do you see you can't stop us?" Sarah asked the old man, and he nodded. "All right, then," Sarah said. "Let him go."

B.B. opened his wings and the old man gasped for breath. Quickly, the three of them hurried into the dark space together and found the ledge at the end. B.B. jumped. Then Sarah helped Billy over and jumped in after him.

CHAPTER 30

In the Green Desert

When they came out the other side, Sarah saw nothing but sand stretching for miles. She picked up a handful and let it run through her fingers. It glinted green in the dim light, and Sarah smiled. "It's green," she said. "This must be the Green Desert. Now all we have to do is find the blemmyes." She pulled out the map Edgar had given her, but it was no help. It only showed how Crooked Canyon connected the Green Desert with the Moonlit Sea.

"B.B.," she said, "you're going to have to take us up."

"Both of you?" he asked.

"Do you think you can?"

"I don't know. We could try."

Sarah nodded and helped Billy onto his back, then climbed on the other side. B.B. flapped his wings and they took off. But as soon as they were in the air, they veered to one side and fell to the ground. Sarah helped Billy to his feet.

"I guess you'll have to go alone," she said.

"Go where?"

"Up there. Try to find out where we are. Find the blemmyes."

"What'll you two do?"

"Wait here, I guess. What else can we do?"

B.B. nodded. "I'll come back as soon as I can," he said, and took off into the dark sky.

Sarah didn't know why, but for some reason she expected him to fly to her right. Instead, B.B. flew to her left. She almost called out to him to change direction, but then knew that it wouldn't make much difference. After all, they had no idea where they were. Every direction would have to be checked.

"Come on, Billy," she said. "We might as well sit down."

They had waited for quite some time when Sarah heard a noise in the distance. She stood up and looked in the direction B.B. had flown. But the noise was coming from behind her. She turned around and peered into the distance, searching the sky for any sign of B.B.

Then a flash of light low on the horizon caught her eye and she adjusted her gaze. To see farther, she climbed onto a cluster of rocks and stood on her tiptoes. In the distance she saw what looked like headlights, but they were blue. At once she realized that they were cold-fire torches and that this was the line of cyclopes that had left the Black Iron Prison in search of her. She assumed they were still on their way to the blemmyes. She couldn't believe it had taken them so long to get this far. But as they grew nearer, she saw that the squat creatures were not alone. Between every two of them was a long pole with something tied to it. Although she couldn't tell what was tied to the poles, she guessed it must be captive blemmyes. The one-eyed creatures had apparently already been to the blemmye camp and were now on their way back to the Black Iron Prison.

She heard a flapping behind her and whirled around as B.B. landed. He was crying.

"What is it, B.B.?" she said. "What's wrong?"

"It was terrible," he said. "I found the blemmyes, all right. What's left of them, anyway. Those things attacked them and burned their houses down until there was nothing left. Then they took the few still alive and tied them to poles and carried them off."

Sarah turned around and looked again at the marching line in the distance. They were moving away from them now, back to the Black Iron Prison, where she was sure they would lock the blemmyes up with Edgar and Jeb.

She sat down on the rocks. "There has to be something we can do," she said. "There has to be some other way that we just haven't thought of yet."

"There isn't," B.B. said. "It's over. We can't stop them."

"Don't say that."

"But it's true. I saw what they did to those poor blemmyes. We don't stand a chance."

"What are you saying?" Sarah asked. "You're going to leave? You're going back to your hole in Crooked Canyon to sit there by yourself, always wondering what your real name is?"

B.B.'s shoulders slumped. "No," he said. "You know I can't do that."

"All right, then," Sarah said, and stood up. "How far is the blemmye camp from here?"

"Not far," B.B. said. "There's a ridge over there and the desert drops into a kind of crater."

"Lead the way," she said.

"But why?"

"Because I want to see it for myself."

The three of them started across the desert. Within a few moments, the darkness had swallowed them up, leaving only their footprints behind.

When they reached the ridge and looked down into the crater, Sarah saw why B.B. had been crying. The blemmye

camp was a wreck, riddled with small fires still burning, flickering blue in the dark, sending up smoke the color of the sky.

"So?" B.B. said. "You've seen it for yourself. Now what?"

Sarah had hoped to come up with some ideas on their way to the camp, but she hadn't. Faced with the destruction below her, she felt even less able to think of anything except to wish that she could have done something to prevent it.

She heaved a sigh and was about to tell B.B. she had no idea what to do when a thin voice floated to them across the distance. "Help," it said.

"Did you hear that?" Sarah said.

B.B. and Billy both nodded.

"Please," the voice cried out again. "Help me."

A new sense of purpose flooded Sarah and she started down the side of the crater as fast as she could.

"Wait, Sarah," B.B. called after her. "What if it's a trap?"

Too late to think about that now, Sarah decided. She was already in the open. If guards from the Black Iron Prison had remained behind in the hopes of still catching her, they were about to succeed.

Sarah stopped at the edge of the camp and looked around. "Where are you?" she called out.

"Over here," the voice said, and Sarah saw something new in movement that she had taken for shadows in the blue firelight. She rushed forward and saw a blemmye, his legs trapped under a collapsed rock wall. He was a strange creature, all right, with his head below his shoulders, in his chest, just as Balthazat had told her.

She knelt beside him and tried to lift the wall but couldn't. "I'm not strong enough by myself," she told the blemmye, then got to her feet. She was about to call out for Billy and B.B., but they were already there. "Maybe if my friends help me and we all work together," she said. B.B. and Billy nodded and the three of them each grabbed part of the wall and lifted. Sarah could hardly believe it

when the rock slab moved enough for the blemmye to pull himself out. Once he was clear, they dropped the wall and it thumped to the ground.

"Thank you," the blemmye said. "My name is Anonimo. You are Sarah. You have come here to ask our help in fighting Balthazat."

Sarah frowned. "That's right. How did you know that?"

"We blemmyes can read minds," Anonimo said. He laughed, then winced in pain. "You know that we tried to defeat Balthazat before and failed. He cannot be defeated unless . . ." Anonimo tried to sit up but couldn't. So Sarah knelt quickly to help him.

"Unless what?" she said.

"Unless you have the Undoer."

"The Undoer? What's that?"

"Only those who have seen it know. They say it has the power to undo what has been done. We don't even know if it's real. Maybe it's not. Legend says that Balthazat came into power because he took it from Tantalus."

"Who?"

"He was the King of Scotopia before Balthazat," Anonimo said, coughing thickly. "Leedo was the king before Tantalus, and so on, each one of them taking the throne only after they got the Undoer. It's what we blemmyes hoped to do the first time around. I was to be made king."

"Do you know where we can find the Undoer?"

"No. If I had it, I would never let anyone know where it was. To risk its discovery would mean to risk being dethroned."

"How big is it?"

Anonimo shrugged. "Some say it's bigger than the

sentinels. Some say it's small enough to hold in your hand."

Sarah stood up. She looked at Billy and B.B. "It's our only hope. We have to find the Undoer."

"But Sarah," B.B. said, "didn't you hear him? We don't even know what it looks like. We'll never be able to find it."

"Not without help."

"Who can help us?"

"Jeb. He's lived as Balthazat's servant for two years."

Anonimo's eyes brightened. "And he is now a friend of yours."

Sarah nodded.

Anonimo's eyes dimmed. "But he is in the Black Iron Prison," he said, obviously still reading Sarah's mind. "Then it is hopeless. No one escapes from the Black Iron Prison."

"I did."

Anonimo stared at her. "I see you climbing through the smoke vent from the Blue Suite."

Sarah nodded. "I'll think about the rest of it later. Right now the most important thing to do is to get back there and see if Jeb can tell me where to find the Undoer." Sarah looked at Billy, then at Anonimo. "But we can't all go. B.B. can't carry more than one of us and Anonimo is in no condition to travel. Not yet. Can you take care of my brother while we go find the Undoer?"

Billy pointed at himself and then at Anonimo.

Sarah laughed. "You'll take care of him?" she asked.

Billy nodded and everyone laughed.

"Good enough for me," Sarah said. "Come on, B.B. Let's fly."

CHAPTER 31

Back to the Black Iron Prison

B.B. stepped into the open and stretched his wings. Sarah climbed onto his back, and a moment later, they lifted into the dark and smoky sky. As they rose higher and higher, Sarah glanced back at the small flickering blue fires. They looked like stars at the bottom of the ocean.

"Which way?" B.B. called.

Sarah pointed in the direction that the cyclops had headed, and B.B. picked up speed.

They soon spotted the flat, bright Moonlit Sea, and against it, the shadow of the Black Iron Prison. Far to the left, Sarah saw the line of marching one-eyed creatures, their torches like a broken sapphire necklace against the shadow-stained green sand. She was glad to see they hadn't made it all the way back yet. She asked B.B. to fly faster.

They soon swooped low over the roof of the Black Iron Prison, and Sarah pointed at the smoke vent she had used for her escape. B.B. pulled his wings back and they landed right next to it.

Sarah got down from B.B.'s back and peered onto the platform below. It was empty. Then she remembered that Edgar had said they would send everybody to search for her. She didn't think he really meant everyone, but she looked into the distance anyway and quickly counted the torches. She stopped at thirty. Maybe they really had sent everyone and the Black Iron Prison was empty except for the prisoners.

"Change of plans," Sarah said. "Get us down to that door."

B.B. nodded and Sarah held on as he flapped up, then swooped down, landing on the cold, flat iron platform. She jumped off B.B. and went to the door. It was open. "Hurry," she said. "Follow me."

Sarah knew she shouldn't be afraid. Still, just being back inside the Black Iron Prison was enough to make her shudder. At first, she couldn't remember how to get to the Blue Suite, but then she remembered that around every corner, the one-eyed guards had gone down the stairs. Sarah tried to move more quickly, but B.B. was having a hard time on the narrow stairs.

"Go back outside and wait," she said. "If the guards reach the prison walls and I'm not back, scream."

B.B. nodded and turned around. Sarah hurried onward, deeper into the gloom.

When at last she reached the door to the Blue Suite, she pounded on it. "Jeb? Edgar? Are you still in there?"

"Sarah?" Jeb called to her through the door. "Is that really you?"

"Of course it's me."

"What's going on? Have you brought the blemmyes?"

"No. Just me. No time for anything but to get you two out of here."

"I'm alone."

"What about Edgar?"

"They took him somewhere else," Jeb said. "I don't know where."

Sarah backed away from the door. She took the key down from its hook on the wall and opened the door to the Blue Suite.

Jeb came out smiling as much as he could with only half a face. "I can't believe you really made it," he said. Then he looked at her and asked, "Where's my face?"

Sarah looked at the floor. "Slight complication," she said.

"Oh, no," Jeb whispered. "I trusted you."

"I know you did. But it wasn't my fault. There was an accident."

Jeb hung his head and turned away slowly. "Do you have any idea where it is?"

"I don't think it matters," Sarah said.

"Of course it matters!" Jeb said. His face was suddenly as angry as it had been in the moment before he had spit in the guard's face.

"Not if we have the Undoer."

"The what?"

"The Undoer. I don't know what it looks like. It could be big or it could be small."

"What are you talking about?" Jeb asked.

"It's what makes Balthazat king. It's part of what gives him his power. It can undo anything that he has done."

Jeb lifted his head slowly, the anger draining away. "Really?"

Sarah nodded. "Did you ever see Balthazat with it?"

Jeb shrugged. "What does it look like?"

"I don't know."

Jeb thought for a minute. "Well, one time, I came into the main room when I hadn't been called. I saw Balthazat playing with something that looked like a pen made of glass. At first he seemed very upset that I had seen him with it. Then he said he could make it as if I had never seen it, if he wanted to. He waved the glass pen around for a minute. But nothing happened. Then he laughed and told me to get out. Do you think that could be what you're talking about?"

Sarah nodded. "Do you know where he keeps it?"

"Yes. A few months later, I was looking for a way to open the box with my face in it. I found the glass pen. I thought he had lost it, but then I realized he had hidden it there."

"In the cabin?"

Jeb nodded.

"Then we have to hurry. Come on."

"What about Edgar?"

"We'll have to come back for him. The guards are almost here."

Sarah ran back upstairs and Jeb followed.

When they got back to the platform, B.B. was gone.

"Oh, no," Sarah gasped. "Where is he?"

"Who?"

"B.B."

"Who's that?"

"A friend. I met him after I left here." Sarah tilted her head back, searching the sky above.

"Why are you looking up there?"

"Because B.B. can fly."

"What?"

"He's a bat. A giant bat. Sort of. The part that isn't a bat is a boy."

"You're not making much sense."

"It will in a minute," Sarah said, and ran toward the wall. She found a ladder and climbed to the outer ledge of the building. When she looked down, she saw guards clustered at the base of the Black Iron Prison. B.B. was circling them, swooping down, picking up rocks and dropping them. He was doing it, Sarah now realized, to keep the guards from getting back inside. But she didn't need him to do that anymore.

"B.B.," she shouted.

He pulled out of a dive-bomb maneuver and flapped up to land near them. The guards, sensing their opportunity, swarmed through the gate, into the prison.

"This way," Sarah shouted, and ran to the wall overlooking the Moonlit Sea.

Jeb looked over the edge and down. "What now?"

"Jump," Sarah said.

"Are you crazy?" Jeb asked.

"It's how I got away before. And if I can do it, you can."

Jeb looked over the edge again and shook his head. "I don't think so."

Sarah laughed.

"What are you laughing at?" Jeb asked.

"It's just that when I was up here before, I wished you were with me so that we could jump together. Now you're chickening out."

"I'm not chicken," Jeb said.

"Then let's go," Sarah said, grabbing Jeb's hand and pulling as hard as she could. He screamed as they sailed through the air and splashed into the Moonlit Sea. Sarah paddled to the surface, blowing the moonlight from her mouth.

She looked around for Jeb. When she didn't see him pop up anywhere, she grew frantic.

B.B. swooped down behind her and skimmed across the surface of the sea. "Where is he?"

"I don't know," Sarah said. "I've got to go down and look for him!"

"We don't have much time," B.B. said. "As soon as the guards realize where you went, they'll come back down."

Sarah nodded and turned over, diving down through the moonlight, scooping through it, searching for Jeb. Then she saw a black shape floating ahead and she paddled faster. By the time she reached him, her lungs were about to burst. She grabbed Jeb's leg and pulled him toward the surface. But he was too heavy. She couldn't make it. She had to get back to the surface, even if it meant going alone.

Just then, a shadow dove in front of her. B.B. grabbed Jeb and swam back toward the top. Sarah paddled as hard as she could and broke through the surface just as B.B. and Jeb did.

She sucked in deep breaths of air as B.B. flew in a circle over her, still holding Jeb. Then she saw the guards on the ledge, looking down and pointing. Sarah knew it wouldn't take them long to reorganize and make their way down. "Take Jeb to shore," she shouted to B.B. "Then come back and get me."

Without answering her, B.B. flew off fast as Sarah paddled toward the beach.

She looked over her shoulder and saw the guards leaving the ledge. She was thankful that none of them had enough courage to jump in after her.

Before she even reached the beach, the first guards came through the door at the base of the Black Iron Prison and ran across the sand. B.B. came just in time, swooping down to pluck her from the sea like a bird of prey with a fish. She caught her breath as they darted into the dark sky, the moonlight streaming from her body, the guards' shouts of anger growing fainter.

CHAPTER 32

Searching for the Undoer

B.B. set Sarah down next to Jeb, who was still unconscious. "Jeb," she said as she rolled him over and started shaking him. "Wake up, Jeb. Wake up." He coughed and moonlight came out of his mouth. A wave of worry swept over her. She hoped he hadn't swallowed any. When he finally blinked and sat up, Sarah heaved a sigh of relief.

"Sarah?" Jeb asked weakly. "Are we dead?"

Sarah laughed, shaking her head. Without thinking, she reached out and pulled Jeb to her, hugging him tightly. But her happiness didn't last long.

"Look!" B.B. shouted, and Sarah turned around. The guards had shifted course and were now coming straight toward them. They weren't very far away, either. Sarah got to her feet and pulled Jeb up.

"B.B., take Jeb, fly ahead and put him down, then come

back for me. We'll have to do it a couple of times to get ahead of the guards, but it's the only way."

"It's not the only way," B.B. said. "Grab on to my feet."

"We tried that before. You can't do it."

"We have to try again."

Sarah looked over her shoulder. The guards were much closer than she had realized. They were bearing down fast, so close that she could see their eyes gleaming in the light of their cold-fire torches.

"Now!" B.B. shouted, and took off into the sky. Sarah and Jeb each reached up and grabbed a foot as B.B. zoomed overhead, jerking them into the sky just in time. The guards were so close Sarah felt their hands on her legs and feet, trying to grab hold. She screamed, pulling her feet up as B.B. flapped his wings harder still and they rose into the sky a bit higher. Just when she thought they were actually going to get away, they suddenly veered to the left. Sarah was certain they would crash back to the ground. But B.B. kept flapping, and in a few more moments, they were high enough for him to glide.

Sarah heaved another sigh of relief.

"I don't know how much longer I can keep this up," B.B. said, and Sarah looked over her shoulder at the ground below. Their distance from the guards was increasing fast, but the guards weren't giving up—they were still coming after them.

"Just a little bit longer," Sarah said.

B.B. kept flying until the torches were like pinpoints behind them. He started to descend, and as they neared the ground, Sarah and Jeb both let go. B.B. landed hard and immediately collapsed to the ground and rolled over, breathing heavily.

Sarah got up and ran to him. Jeb followed her slowly. "You did it, B.B. You did it!"

B.B. smiled between deep breaths. He tried to answer with words but couldn't. So he nodded instead.

Sarah pulled out the map Edgar had given her and unfolded it. As she had hoped, it showed that the edge of the Forest of Shadows was just ahead. She didn't know exactly how far it was, but at least she could tell they were headed in the right direction.

"We've got to keep moving. We'll be safe once we get to the Forest of Shadows. I'm sure of it."

"And what about the sentinels?" Jeb asked.

"If Balthazat has already found another way through from Penumbra, then I'm sure he doesn't care much about us. As far as he's concerned, he already got what he wanted. He doesn't think we can stop him."

"He may be right."

"No," Sarah said. "I won't let him get away with it." She went to B.B. and helped him up. "B.B.," she said, "you need to fly ahead of us. Make sure we keep going in the right direction. See how close we are. Keep looking for sentinels or anything else that might get in our way."

"Wait," Jeb said. "I'm pretty sure Balthazat's cabin is far from the Black Iron Prison. It could take us hours to walk all the way back. By then it really could be too late. Why don't I just tell you where the—what did you call it?"

"The Undoer?"

"Right—the Undoer. Why don't I just tell you where it is and B.B. can fly you to the cabin instead?"

Sarah shook her head. "You're the one who's seen it. B.B. should take you to get it."

"But what about you?"

"I'll keep going this way," Sarah said. "As soon as you find the Undoer, you bring it back to me."

"And what then?" Jeb asked. "We don't even know how to use it."

"That doesn't matter right now. As long as we have it, at least we can be sure that Balthazat won't be able to use it." Then Sarah smiled as something else occurred to her. "Maybe we can even use it to force Balthazat to do what we want."

"All right," Jeb said, and faced B.B. "Are you ready?"

B.B. nodded tiredly, turning around so that Jeb could climb onto his back. Sarah waved as they took off, then followed them as quickly as she could on foot. In no time, they melted into the darkness, shadows swallowed by shadows. Sarah put her head down and picked up her pace.

She thought about all the things that would have to be undone once they had the Undoer. She would have to put Jeb's face together. Get Edgar out of the Black Iron Prison. Restore the blemmye camp. Give Billy his mouth back. Make B.B. a normal boy again. And, of course, send the sleeping souls back to Penumbra, if indeed Balthazat had really stolen any. The last thing she would undo was her visit to Scotopia. Then she could keep the Undoer and ensure that Balthazat's power would be incomplete.

Jeb was right, though: none of them knew how to use the Undoer. Sarah tried to think who could help them with that. She knew that Balthazat certainly wouldn't tell her, even if she could find out where he was and ask him. Anonimo didn't know how to use it, even though he had planned to get it. He wasn't even sure it was real. The only people who would know how to use it, she realized, were those who had used it before. Anonimo had mentioned other kings, like Tantalus and Leedo. Sarah wondered if they were still alive. She supposed that if they were, they would most likely be in the Black Iron Prison, and she shuddered at the thought of going back there again.

Sarah was thinking so hard about these things that she

almost didn't see the gaping hole in front of her. At the last possible moment, she stopped herself short and pulled back. As she did, she stumbled and started to fall backward. Pinwheeling her arms, she threw herself sideways, along the edge of the hole. Grabbing at the ground, she barely managed to hold on. Carefully, she pulled herself away from the edge. Once she was clear, she climbed back to her feet and turned around. The hole wasn't just a hole, it was a gigantic canyon of darkness that stretched almost as far as she could see. She would have to follow the edge to find a way around it. She decided to head to her left, toward the Moonlit Sea.

After ten minutes of following the canyon's edge, Sarah realized she was way out of line with her original path. This meant that when B.B. returned, he would have a hard time finding her. She decided she should just go back to where she had started. But when she did, she saw a thin line of glowing blue torches in the distance. She couldn't believe the guards had caught up with her so quickly. She looked around, trying to figure out what she could do to avoid capture. The most obvious answer also seemed to be the most difficult: she had to hide in the black chasm.

She went to the edge and peered over. What little she could see was very steep. In a few spots, however, she saw enough rocky outcroppings to make her believe she

could climb down and bury herself in the shadows until the guards had passed. She took one last glance over her shoulder to make sure they weren't close enough to see her, then climbed into the chasm, lowering herself into the shadows as carefully as she could.

In a few moments, she heard the guards tramping over the black sand, kicking some of it over the edge. When they passed Sarah, the sand fell on her like stinging rain. Some of it got into her eyes, and she rubbed them furiously. Just when she thought it couldn't get any worse, some of the sand got into her nose and mouth and she felt a violent sneeze clawing its way out of her. Before she could stop it, the sneeze exploded from her. She froze.

So did the guards.

CHAPTER 33

The Tables Are Turned

Sarah dared herself to look up. She saw the glow of their torches just over the chasm's edge and heard several of the creatures speaking in harsh whispers. Then one of them called for quiet.

The glow brightened as they all moved toward the edge in a line and looked down. They lowered their torches slowly, and Sarah watched in terror as the shadows around her melted away.

When at last the cold blue light reached her, she could think of nothing else to do but scream at the top of her lungs. To her surprise, the piercing shriek she let out so frightened the guards that the one nearest to her stumbled and fell. He dropped his torch as he made a frantic attempt to grab on to something—anything—but he missed, and as he plummeted into the pit, Sarah looked down. The chasm was so dark that he vanished from sight almost instantly.

His torch, however, continued glowing even as it got smaller and smaller. Sarah was still screaming when she faced the edge again.

The other guards were crowding in, pointing at Sarah and shouting. Several of them began working together, holding on to each other to form a chain so they could reach her. Sarah didn't know which way to go. She screamed yet again, and just then, a black shape appeared, knocking into the guard at the top of the chain, toppling him over. The rest went with him, a half-dozen guards in all, tumbling down the way the first one had gone. Sarah flattened herself against the chasm wall as they whooshed past her.

She heard more confused shouts above, and when she looked up she saw the black shape gliding along the edge of the chasm, knocking the guards over like dominoes. As the shape passed directly overhead, she saw that it was B.B., with Jeb hanging on underneath, using his feet to kick the guards in.

As soon as it was clear, Sarah pulled herself up. She looked around—they had gotten every guard but one. He was running away from the chasm, back the way he had come. B.B. dropped Jeb and swerved sharply, tearing after the fleeing guard. The cyclops looked over his shoulder and, when he saw B.B. bearing down on him, threw his torch down and ran faster. But B.B. was too fast, and he snatched the guard up in his claws and lifted him off the ground. Sarah watched as B.B. flew toward the chasm, obviously planning to drop the guard in with the others.

"Wait!" Sarah shouted. "Don't drop him in. We need him!"

Jeb grabbed Sarah. "Are you crazy? What are you talking about? I found the Undoer."

"And maybe he can help us with it."

Jeb's eyes widened and he shouted with Sarah, "Stop, B.B.! Don't drop him in!"

B.B. was already over the chasm when he banked and flew back toward them, the guard still in his claws. He dropped the guard on the ground next to them, then landed and started waddling back.

The one-eyed creature shook with fear. "Please don't hurt me," he said, his voice weak and thin.

"We won't," Sarah said, "if you help us."

"Anything," the guard said.

"Do you know where we can find Tantalus or Leedo?"

The guard's one eye widened.

"Who are they?" Jeb asked.

"Kings before Balthazat," Sarah said. "They know how to use the Undoer." Jeb smiled and Sarah looked back at the guard.

But he was gone.

Sarah heard something at her back, and when she turned around, she saw the guard running toward the chasm edge. "Stop him, B.B.!" she shouted.

B.B. flapped his wings and took off, but not before the guard reached the edge and jumped. As the creature vanished from sight, B.B. dove after him. Sarah heard B.B. squealing, using his radar to find the falling guard in the dark. She held her breath until she couldn't hold it anymore. When she finally let it out, B.B. burst from the chasm, the guard squirming in his claws. Sarah and Jeb jumped for joy as he brought the guard back to them and dropped him on the ground.

Sarah looked at Jeb. "So let's see it," she said. Jeb reached into his pocket. He took out the Undoer and held it up. It was just as he had described: like a pen made of glass. Only, it was far more beautiful than Sarah had expected. Even in the darkness it seemed to glow with a faintly shifting purple light. Sarah took it from Jeb's hand and showed it to the guard.

"Do you know what this is?" she asked.

The guard's lips trembled as he nodded.

"Tell me," Sarah said.

"The . . . the Undoer," said the guard, his voice a mere whisper.

Sarah nodded. "That's right. And we intend to use it so that Balthazat will be powerless again. That's why we need Tantalus or Leedo. They know how to use it."

"That's true," the guard said as he got to his feet and dusted himself off. "But talking to them won't do any good."

"Why not?"

"Because they can't answer. Balthazat took their mouths."

Sarah's shoulders sagged.

"Could they write down how to use it?" Jeb asked.

The guard shook his head. "Balthazat took their hands, too. That's the way it is with everyone down there."

"Down where?"

"Where they are: in the bottom of the Black Iron Prison."

Sarah grimaced. No wonder the guard was so scared of Balthazat. She didn't even want to think about being locked up in the dark without a mouth or hands.

"Oh, well," Jeb said. "I guess that's that."

"No," Sarah said, facing Jeb angrily. "It can't be. We've got to think. There must be some other way we can find out how to use it."

"You heard him," Jeb said. "They can't talk. They can't write. This whole thing has been hopeless from the beginning. I don't know why I ever thought anything would come of it. I let you get my hopes up. And now I see the way it really is."

Sarah shook her head at Jeb. "You've been here too long," she said.

"What's that supposed to mean?"

"You're giving up too easily," she said. "Just when I need you the most. That's not what friends do."

Jeb looked away, unable to meet Sarah's gaze, obviously ashamed. "Are you always this right?"

"No," Sarah said. "I just happen to be this time. Now we've got to think. There has to be a way we can get what we need from Tantalus and Leedo." Sarah closed her eyes and turned the problem over in her head. Then, instead of focusing on what the former kings couldn't do, she decided to think about what they *could* do. All at once it hit her, and she snapped her fingers. "Wait a second," she said. "Can they think?"

"What?" Jeb said, completely confused.

She grabbed the guard. "Can they think?"

"I don't know," the guard said. "I guess so."

She released him and faced Jeb and B.B. "That's it. All we need to do is have them think about how to use the Undoer."

"And what good will that do?"

"Because we'll have Anonimo with us," she said. "He can read minds, remember?" Jeb and B.B. smiled. She told B.B. to go to the blemmye camp and tell Anonimo and Billy what had happened. "Then lead them back to the Black Iron Prison," Sarah said. "We should get there about the same time you do."

B.B. nodded and took off.

Sarah pushed the guard forward, then grabbed Jeb's hand and pulled him into the dark.

CHAPTER 34

Using the Undoer

Sarah was right: they all reached the Black Iron Prison at almost the same time. She was glad to see Anonimo and B.B., but she was especially glad to see Billy, and she hugged him tightly before she realized what she was doing. He pushed her away, then tapped Anonimo on the shoulder and pointed at his own head.

Anonimo laughed. "He says, 'Yuck. What's wrong with you?'"

Sarah smiled. She faced Billy and shrugged. "I guess I'm actually glad to see you," she said. "As hard as that is to believe."

Anonimo read Billy's mind again, then said: "He says, 'Whatever.'"

"Not much longer now," she whispered to him, "and you'll have your mouth back. I promise." He nodded his understanding.

Sarah faced the guard. "Will you have any problem getting us in there?"

"No," the guard said. "I'm the only one left now." And with that, he turned and led them through the gate, into the prison.

Inside, the halls glowed with light from rows of cold-fire torches. The guard wound through a series of narrowing passages and down steep staircases until at last he stopped outside a tall thin door.

"This is it," he said. "The bottom. They're all in there."

"Okay," Sarah said. "Open it up."

The guard nodded and took a key from around his neck. He slipped it into the lock and twisted it. The lock opened with a clunk. He pulled the handle and the door swung open with a shrieking creak. Rust dust floated down, glinting in the blue light like copper snow. Stale air wafted out at them from the darkness beyond.

Behind her, Anonimo moaned, as if in pain.

"What is it?" Sarah asked.

"So much suffering in there," he said. "I don't think I can go in. Not unless some of them calm themselves."

Sarah faced the darkness and shuddered. She was glad she couldn't read minds the way Anonimo could.

"I'll go in and bring them out," she said. She motioned

for the guard to get a torch and come with her. "Do you know their names?" she asked him.

The guard shook his head. "No. I've only ever been in there once. That was enough."

"Give me the torch, then," Sarah said.

"I'll do it," a voice said, and Sarah whirled around to find Edgar standing in the doorway.

She couldn't believe her eyes. Until now, she had really been having some doubts about whether or not they could make this work. Seeing Edgar, though, changed that. Now that he was here, she was sure they could do it. "Edgar," she said. "This is where they took you?"

Edgar nodded. "Once they found out you were missing, they tried to make me tell where you had gone. When I refused, they put me in here."

Sarah smiled and hugged him. "Thank you," she said. "For not telling."

"No," Edgar said. "Thank you. For coming to my rescue. I'm afraid they had in mind to take my mouth after all." He reached up and took a torch down from the wall. "So who are you looking for?"

"Tantalus," Jeb said.

"Or Leedo," Sarah added.

Edgar nodded and stepped back through the door. It

looked to Sarah as if he were being swallowed by an iron giant's gaping toothless mouth.

They all waited in breathless silence, watching the dark. Sarah heard Edgar moving about, calling out for Tantalus and Leedo. Every so often, she saw his torch flicker past. At last he emerged, dragging with him a poor pale creature with no mouth and no hands. His clothes were tattered and moth-eaten. His gray hair and bushy beard were like silver wire. His skin was so pale and pasty that Sarah thought it looked like cooked spaghetti. She wondered how long he had been in there, then decided she didn't want to know. He blinked at the light and stared at them all.

"I'm fairly certain this is Leedo," Edgar said.

The old man nodded.

Sarah stepped closer to him. "It's okay," she said. "We're here to help you."

Leedo looked at her suspiciously, between darting glances at the others in the corridor.

Sarah took the Undoer from her pocket and held it up. "Do you see this?"

Leedo's eyes widened and he reached for it reflexively. Obviously he had forgotten that he didn't have hands. When he saw the stumps, he froze and stared at them. After a moment, he dropped his arms to his side and bowed his head.

"Help me to use this and I'll give you your hands back," Sarah said.

Leedo looked at her and pointed at his mouthless face with one handless stump.

"I know," Sarah said. She motioned for Anonimo to come forward. "This is Anonimo," she continued. "He's a blemmye. He can hear what you're thinking."

Leedo lunged for Anonimo, staring him in the eyes, obviously thinking at him as hard as he could.

Anonimo stumbled backward. "Yes, yes," he said. "It's true. I can read minds and we are here to help you. Now calm down."

Leedo backed away and nodded.

"Clearly and carefully," Sarah told him, "I need you to tell Anonimo how to use the Undoer. Just think it through step by step."

Leedo nodded slowly and closed his eyes. His breathing was shallow and rapid.

Anonimo took a deep breath and bowed his head in concentration, listening intently. Then, very quietly, he said, "First, you must clear your mind. Then you must picture exactly what it is you want to undo. Then, when you are sure you are thinking of nothing else, say the following words:

"What has been done

I now undo

By counting two one

And then one two."

Sarah felt the Undoer growing warmer and she held it up. The purple light inside wasn't faint anymore. It had grown in strength, as if it was closer to the surface than it had been before.

Leedo snapped his eyes open and held his stumps out to Sarah.

"Hold on," she said. "First things first." Sarah turned away from Leedo and went to her brother. She knelt in front of him and closed her eyes. Concentrating as hard as she could on seeing his mouth back on his face, she lifted the Undoer and said:

"What has been done
I now undo

By counting two one
And then one two."

Sarah was terrified. What if the Undoer hadn't worked? What if she had somehow done it wrong? She sucked in a deep breath and slowly opened her eyes.

CHAPTER 35

What Was Undone and What Wasn't

"You did it, Sarah!" Billy said. "You really did it!"

Sarah couldn't believe it. The Undoer had worked! Billy's mouth was back on his face and he was talking with it.

"I'm talking," Billy said. "I'm actually talking!"

Sarah hugged her brother tightly. And this time, he hugged her back. He didn't say "Yuck" or "What's wrong with you?" And Sarah didn't mind at all.

She felt a hand on her shoulder and turned to find Jeb staring at her with a hungry look in his eye.

Sarah smiled at him. Again she closed her eyes and concentrated. Again she said the words, and again she felt the Undoer get warmer.

When she opened her eyes, she saw that Jeb was crying. His face was whole now, and he rubbed it with both hands, feeling both cheeks, both eyes, both ears. "I don't know how I can ever thank you," he said.

"You don't need to thank me," Sarah said. "I couldn't have done it without you."

"Can I be next, please?" B.B. said.

Sarah faced him and nodded. "Of course, B.B.," she said, and closed her eyes. She held B.B. in her mind and then spoke the words again:

"What has been done
   I now undo
   By counting two one
   And then one two."

When she opened her eyes, B.B. wasn't a giant bat anymore; he was a little boy in a bat costume. He looked down at himself and said, "My name is Joshua Turner." He looked at Sarah. "My name is Joshua Turner," he said again as if it was the best news he had ever heard in his life. "I remember now. It was Halloween. I was at my grandma's house. We had read a story in school about a house with secret passages and doors in it and I was just playing around and I pulled the bookcase out and I thought it was a real secret passage and I went through it and I came here and I found Balthazat, who said he was the King of the Cats, but he tricked me and tried to make me take him back, but I couldn't find my way, so he punished me by taking away my memory and turning me into a bat."

"It's okay, B.B." Sarah said, and laughed. "Joshua, I

mean. It's almost all over now. You'll be home soon and everything will be back the way it was."

Joshua nodded. Sarah turned around and faced Leedo.

"All right," she said. "Now you."

Leedo bowed his head and held up his stumps. Sarah closed her eyes and pictured him whole. Again she said the words, and again she felt the Undoer glow warmly in her hand.

When she opened her eyes, Leedo had his hands and mouth back. He touched his lips with his fingers and then opened his eyes and looked at Sarah. He stared at the Undoer in her hand. But there wasn't any joy in his eyes, only a kind of terrible rage. "Give it to me," he shrieked in a voice that sounded like tearing metal. As he lunged at her, Sarah tried to dive out of the way. But she was too late. He crashed into her and they both fell to the floor. Jeb and Joshua grabbed Leedo from behind and tried to pull him off Sarah, but they couldn't. He was much bigger than they were. Edgar came forward to help, but there was no room for him.

"Billy!" Sarah yelled. He looked at her, his eyes going wide. She threw the Undoer to him and he caught it. "Quickly," she said. "Undo him!"

When Leedo saw what Sarah had done, he started to get up. Instead of pulling on him, Jeb and Joshua now sat on him with their full weight, trying to keep him pinned to the ground while Billy closed his eyes and said:

"What once was done

I now undo

By counting down two one

And then one two."

Nothing happened.

"That's not it," Sarah yelled.

Billy opened his eyes, frantic. "I can't remember," he said.

"We can't hold him any longer!" Jeb shouted.

Leedo pushed up as hard as he could and Jeb and Joshua both fell backward, crashing into Edgar and the guard, and knocking them over, too. Sarah, now free, pulled herself up and dove for Billy. She grabbed his hands with both of hers so that each of them was touching the Undoer.

"You think it," she said. "I'll say it."

"Will that work?" he asked.

"We have to try."

Billy closed his eyes and Sarah said:

"What has been done

I now undo

By counting two one

And then one two."

There was a sudden flash of light brighter than anything

she had ever seen. For a moment, Sarah thought a bolt of lightning had shot through the ceiling. She and Billy both fell over and went into a spin. She tried to hold on to him, but something started to pull them apart. Then she saw the others spinning around them at the same time, as if they were all caught in a whirlpool of light.

Then everything came apart. Leedo whooshed away first, shooting through the brightness until he vanished from sight and all that was left of him was his voice, screaming "Nooo!" Anonimo followed right behind him, and just as fast, he, too, was gone. Then Edgar whirled past Sarah. When their eyes met, he said, "Oh, dear," and zipped away as if he had been launched from a slingshot. Joshua flew by next, flapping the wings of his Halloween costume as hard as he could, but it was no use. Like the others, he shot off into the light and was gone. Finally Jeb launched off, his eyes wide, his mouth open. But his face was still all there.

Sarah didn't understand what was happening. She looked down and saw that she and Billy were still holding on to each other, the Undoer between them. She didn't know for how much longer, though. Even now, their grip was slipping. Then Sarah felt a hand grab her arm and she saw Balthazat behind her. Only, he hadn't bothered with the cat disguise. His hair was smoke and his eyes were fire and his mouth glowed like Fourth of July fireworks.

"What have you done?" he roared.

"Not what we've done!" Sarah shouted. "What we've undone."

She felt Billy's hand slip from her fingers and both of

them whooshed away. Suddenly, darkness surrounded her as completely as the light had only a moment before.

She kicked her feet and flailed her arms and all at once her covers flew off and she was in her bedroom, back in her bed.

She froze, catching her breath. For a long time, she remained perfectly still, staring at the moonlit ceiling. Then she heard footsteps in the hall, outside her room. The door opened and Billy came in, rubbing his eyes.

Sarah sat up and looked at him. "Billy," she said, "are you all right?"

He nodded. "Did everything that I think just happened really happen?"

Now it was Sarah's turn to nod. "What were you thinking when we used the Undoer?"

"Just that I wanted everyone to go back where they belonged."

Sarah smiled. "That must be what happened," she said. "Everyone went home." Sarah looked at the clock now and saw that it was almost 3:00 a.m.

Billy took another step into her room. "What about Balthazat?"

Sarah shrugged. "I guess he must be back in his cabin."

"What about the Undoer?"

"I thought you had it," Sarah said.

Billy shook his head. "I thought you had it."

"I wish," Sarah said. "There are some things around here that I'd like to undo."

"Like me, I suppose?" Billy asked.

Sarah laughed. "Nope. Believe it or not, I think you did okay. All things considered."

"Really?"

"Really."

"So what do we do now?"

"Go back to sleep," Sarah said. "I'm exhausted."

"But if Balthazat is back in his cabin, that means he'll still be trying to find a way through. We have to go back and stop him."

Sarah twisted her hair. "I don't know. If we go behind the bookcase again, something worse might happen this time."

"Can't be any worse than what Balthazat is trying to do," Billy said.

Sarah nodded. "You're right about that."

Just then, they heard a loud banging downstairs. Sarah and Billy looked at each other. Then Sarah looked at the clock. It was exactly three o'clock. "Oh, no," she said. "The sleepers." Quickly, she jumped out of bed and dropped to her knees. "I hope you didn't undo this," she said, shoving her hands under the mattress and pulling out the journal and the key. "Phew," she said as she got to her feet and started for the door.

"Wait," Billy said. "Where are you going?"

"Downstairs to let the dead in."

"But what about Mom and Dad?"

"I guess they're in for a big surprise."

Billy smiled. "Wait for me," he said. "This I gotta see."

Together, the two of them ran downstairs.

Acknowledgments

Thanks to Betty Habel and Cynthia Metcalf, my fourth-grade teachers, for starting all this publishing stuff. Thanks to Rick Hautala, the rainmaker; Christopher Golden, the connection; Stephanie Elliott, the chance-taker; Jenny Bent, the negotiator; Kelly Murphy, the vision-painter; Krista Vitola, the wise reader; and Françoise Bui, my guiding hand. Thanks to my children for being kids, even when I wish they'd grow up. And thanks especially to my wife, Kristie, for sticking with me in spite of all those rejection letters.

About the Author

Mark Steensland was born and raised in California. He self-published his first book when he was in fourth grade and has been telling stories ever since—some of them true. He became a professional journalist at the age of eighteen, writing about movies for such magazines as *Prevue* and *American Cinematographer*. He has also written, directed, and produced numerous award-winning films that have played in festivals around the world. He lives in Erie, Pennsylvania, with his wife, their three children, a dog, and a cat he is fairly certain is not Balthazat. *Behind the Bookcase* is his first novel. Find out more at whatisbehindthebookcase.com.